Rediscovery

Val Case

ISBN: 978-0-6481726-8-0

 A catalogue record for this book is available from the National Library of Australia

Layout and design by Level Heading (levelheading.com.au)

ACKNOWLEDGEMENTS

These stories were written a few years ago and came to light when clearing out some cupboards. On re-reading and revising, there seemed to be a possible thematic connection, hence the title.

Some of these have been read in the past by various individuals whose comments or criticism have been helpful and are recognised. Of late I have benefited from the assistance of long-time friend, Ray Radford, particularly in regard to the illustrations. To Bernie Schultz of Level Heading, my gratitude for the skills demonstrated in the development of this small book, including the editing, formatting and cover design. He has created a reality from my rather vague initial suggestion for which I sincerely thank him.

ABOUT THE AUTHOR

Born in Skipton (Vic) in 1937, Val Case has worked as a nurse and social worker in Australia, U.S. and England before retiring to Castlemaine in 2009. Her first novel, *The Undertaker's Wife*, was published in 2014, and she is currently working on the sequel, *The Undertaker's Daughter*.

CONTENTS

It's all in the Mind

Normally the long drive from metropolitan Melbourne to her old home town of Yarrawonga was one Susie enjoyed, particularly the change, over distance, from crowded city to sparsely-populated flat countryside. Not so today, though. It wasn't the heat either as her vehicle had air conditioning of sorts.

The big problem occupying her mind and shutting out awareness of the trip was the fact of her mother's birthday. Tomorrow. Not any old birthday, either. It was a milestone one – she would be fifty. Clearly something special was required. It should have been easy, it always was in the past. Mum liked pretty things. She always responded with delight to jewellery or perfume.

Something told her this birthday would be different. There was definite irritability in her mother's voice when Susie rang home last week to tell them that she could make the visit.

'Don't worry about the birthday. I don't want anything. It's bad enough being over the hill without everyone fussing. I'd rather just forget about it.'

Luckily, Dad answered the phone when Susie rang a few days later, giving her the opportunity to ask whether her mother was all right.

'Well, no, since you ask. She isn't. She's been real hard to live with lately. I can't do anything right, no matter how hard

I try. It's good you're coming up, maybe you can talk some sense into her.'

Susie had smiled to herself. Dad was a typical honest Aussie bloke who didn't pretend to understand women. All in all, though, theirs seemed like a normal marriage, reasonably comfortable without any major stresses. Years ago she'd asked why she didn't have any brothers or sisters. Mum had taken her into their bedroom and shut the door. With some discomfort she had explained about the several miscarriages she had suffered.

'We'd get our hopes up, but it wasn't to be. That's why you are so special to us.'

But now the onset of the unwelcome change of life was obviously affecting her. I'll get her to see the GP, Susie decided. There is help available, but I'll have to approach it sensitively.

Soon the flat pasture gave way to the outskirts of the major inland town of Shepparton. She stopped for a coffee in the main street and spent about twenty minutes in various gift shops in a fruitless search for inspiration.

The last fifty kilometres brought her to the outskirts of Yarrawonga, known as one of Victoria's charming river towns. The new leisure centre was on her right. A welcome addition to the town's amenities, she'd heard it was proving popular with both locals and tourists. Outside, a new placard caught her eye: 'Have a Float!' it invited. Fantastic, thought Susie. He's put in a flotation tank – full marks for initiative! Although they had sprung up in many suburbs in Melbourne, Susie certainly didn't expect to find one here.

Almost as soon as she decided to make an appointment for herself there and then, the thought flashed into her mind: What about Mum? It would be a very different present from the usual wrapped offering, but it might, just might, work for her. I bet the possibility has never crossed her mind, she mused. She will probably need quite a lot of persuasion. Well, here goes.

Above the counter was a 1990 calendar with February 10th circled in red. The manager noted her glance. Yes, he'd only installed the tanks a couple of weeks ago. Bookings were coming in, but slowly. He could offer a range of times for tomorrow.

Susie glanced at the shelf on which sat a cassette container. 'Are those tapes?' she asked

'Yes, the subliminal type. Some people, especially from the city, ask for a specific one when they're having a float. We've got several themes: stop smoking, lose weight, be more positive, deal with anxiety – that sort of thing.'

'This will be for my mother, a birthday present with a difference. She's been a bit edgy lately, the anti-anxiety tape might help here. But I wouldn't mention it to her, she is just as likely to call it brainwashing.'

The manager laughed.

'I understand. It's so subtle that she won't be aware of it, but a couple of people have claimed good success from that one.'

'Good. I'll order it. The main problem is going to be getting her to take the plunge, so to speak. I've had lots of floats myself and can assure her that it's okay.'

'I've got two tanks, quite separate of course. Would you like to book the same time? What about two o'clock tomorrow?'

Susie agreed and decided on a wellbeing tape for herself. A swipe of the card, and the booking was completed. Conscious of the time, she declined his invitation to inspect the premises, taking instead the descriptive pamphlet outlining the philosophy of flotation and the actual procedure involved.

As she pulled up in the familiar drive, her mother appeared at the front door. Her first words weren't promising.

'You could have rung me. I didn't know when you were coming.'

Susie attempted an embrace but found the older woman's body stiff and resistant.

'It's all right, Mum! It's only me, not the Queen. Lovely to see you. I'm dying for a cuppa.'

Later, having dumped her overnight bag on her old bed, she sat at the kitchen table facing her mother with the familiar teapot between them. To Susie's relief, a brief wry smile appeared on Beth Hawkin's face when she was asked whether she was looking forward to her birthday tomorrow.

'Has Dad organised anything?'

'I hope not!' her mother retorted. 'I told him I don't want any fuss. Who wants to celebrate getting old. It's bad enough being three years older than him – turning fifty makes it even worse.'

'I'm sure he doesn't see it like that,' Susie suggested tentatively.

Beth snorted.

'He's been getting on my nerves so much lately I wish he'd go back to full-time at the Co-op. Do you want to have a shower or anything? I'd better start getting tea ready. Damn those flies.' She swatted vigorously but ineffectually.

The cool, refreshing shower, the languid quiet of the country afternoon and the vaguely realised sense of being home, all contributed to a pleasant sleepiness.

An hour later she woke to a knock.

'Aren't you going to say hello to your old dad?' he said, appearing at the door.

Susie jumped off the bed and gave him a hug. How strong and comforting he felt. Always the same. Not like Mum, lately anyway. With that thought in her mind she broke out of the embrace and looked at him squarely.

'I see what you mean about Mum, she's quite touchy, isn't she? It can't be easy for you.'

'I was hoping you'd speak to her. Get her to see a doctor or something.' Susie nodded. They often met on the same wavelength.

'I agree. Do you know what I'm giving her as a birthday present?'

'No idea – surprise me.'

'I probably will! I'm giving her a float!'

'A – what?'

'I'll have to talk her into it, I realise that. She doesn't know anything about it yet, I thought I'd bring it up over tea. Not only that, I've arranged for a special tape to be played, but she won't know anything about it.'

Roy looked completely bewildered.

'Well, I'll have to trust your judgement. I'd better go and say hello to her or she'll think I'm in here talking about her.'

The meal was predictably plain but satisfying. Susie brought her parents up to date on her work and social activities before broaching the subject of her mother's birthday.

'Mum, I haven't bought you anything ...' she began.

Beth broke in: 'Good. There's nothing I need.'

'But I am going to give you something – an experience. It's something you might not have heard about, it's called a float.'

Both parents looked blank.

'The leisure centre's just installed a couple, you may not have heard about it. They're very popular in Melbourne. I've had quite a few myself and really love what they do for me. Basically it provides an experience of weightlessness and produces sublime relaxation.' She paused, noting the blank expressions but no questions forthcoming yet.

'You go into a tank of water at body temperature which is buoyant like seawater, but more so, and just let yourself go. Mum, I've booked for you and me to have one tomorrow at two o'clock.'

11

There was a brief silence, then Roy spoke.

'How does it work? I mean you float in a swimming pool, I used to as a kid, but this seems well, different ...'

Susie produced the pamphlet and pointed out the features of the flotation tank, the roller door, the shallow pool of warm water saturated with magnesium sulphate, the gentle darkness to encourage relaxation.

'When you adjust to it you lose all track of time and just drift.'

Her voice conveyed the conviction of a true believer. Beth looked uncertain. Clearly this was well outside her comfort zone. She was just at the point of saying she wanted it cancelled when Roy spoke.

'No, Susie, I don't think Mum can handle this sort of thing.'

Immediately, Beth's attitude changed.

'You don't make decisions for me, thank you. Yes, as long as you're there too, Susie, I'll give it a go.'

Susie breathed a sigh of relief and caught her father's eye. To her surprise, he gave her a discreet wink.

Beth accepted the breakfast-in-bed ritual with quite good grace. When the morning post brought several cards and a few little parcels from family and friends, she seemed to be in a reasonably good mood. But by midday, second thoughts surfaced about the afternoon's agenda.

'What if I have a panic attack when I'm shut in that thing?' she demanded.

'Mum, you're in complete control. You can open the roller door if you want to let light in, and there's a button to press if you need help.'

'I don't know. Why couldn't you have given me a box of chocolates?' she asked mournfully.

At ten-to-two Susie parked at the leisure centre and opened the passenger door to let her nervous mother out.

This time the manager's wife was in charge. She wished Beth a happy birthday and, aware that it was her first float, spoke reassuringly to her about the nature of the procedure and what to expect. Susie was glad to note that her mother seemed to respond to the warmly expressed encouragement.

'Susie, you're in Cubicle 2. Do you need any help from me?' asked the manageress. Susie smilingly declined, pleased to see her mother being led to the other private room to be guided through the process.

As for Beth, she felt vulnerable. It took all her self-control to stay, now that Susie had disappeared behind the adjacent door. She had never been particularly brave, she accepted that. It was always easier to say 'no thanks' than to put herself through the stress of coping with something new. She tried to focus on what was in front of her.

The tank itself looked like an egg-shaped igloo. She noted with reluctant approval that everything so far seemed spotlessly clean and smelled fresh. Before leaving quietly, the manageress' instructions had been to undress, take a short shower then lower herself into the interior of the tank. Beth decided to do what she had been told to. Presumably the lady knew what she was talking about.

Soft music played as she gently eased herself into the water. The feeling was quite unfamiliar – her body felt embraced and curiously half-submerged. So this is the float effect, Beth thought, as she adjusted to the environment. As she lowered the roller door the lights dimmed to darkness. It was an unreal sensation – suspended there in water at body temperature with no physical point of reference, no contact. It must be like this in the womb she mused.

The music softened. Beth found herself breathing more slowly and deeply. Squirming around, she felt strangely free and unencumbered.

Then she became aware of the sound of waves with indistinct voices superimposed. She tried to make out what the voices were saying, but they were too faint. I feel I'm floating on a cloud, away from earth, somewhere in the universe.

On the other hand, she was becoming very conscious of herself, her whole body, parts she had not paid attention to for a long time. Her whole being seemed to glow, to pulse, to feel alive. Even her thoughts became sensual, though not distastefully. It was as though some magic was taking place. This could go on forever, she thought wonderingly.

The next awareness was of the dim voices fading, to be replaced by music increasing in volume to a lovely bell-like sound. Light gradually increased and the capsule became visible. There was a double tap on the door. Beth remembered this was the signal to emerge. 'Slowly, gradually, take your time,' had been the advice.

With some reluctance she eased her flaccid body out of the water and was eventually able to stand. A shower, drying off with a snowy white towel and slow redressing followed.

Beth tried to identify the state of her body. All her muscles felt soft, no tension at all. But something else was different. She was acutely aware of her erogenous zones – they actually tingled in an almost forgotten, but immensely pleasurable way.

The manageress looked at her with interest as she entered the reception area.

'You look as though you enjoyed that.'

'It was – it was really amazing,' Beth managed to say.

Turning to her daughter who followed just behind, she clasped her in a warm hug.

'Thank you, darling. It was quite, well, different.'

On the short trip home, neither was inclined to talk. Susie had arranged to have coffee with a friend down town, so she let her mother out at their gate before moving off.

'You might find you want to have a rest after that, people often do.'

A rest was not foremost on Beth's mind at that moment. For the first time in years she wanted her husband. More accurately, she desired her husband.

'Roy?' she called. 'Roy?'

'I'm in the shed. What do you want?' came his voice.

'You. I want you. I'm in the bedroom.'

A surprise greeted him as he opened the door. His wife of nearly thirty years had lowered the blinds and placed a lighted candle on the bedside table. He noticed on his pillow the unused tube of lubricant their GP had recommended some time ago, but, alas, Beth was never 'in the mood.' She was sitting on the bed wearing a flimsy negligee he vaguely remembered from some holiday in the distant past.

Roy looked at his wife with a mixed expression of disbelief and tentative hope. Her face had – there was no other word for it – an eager glow, eyes shining, lips parted. This was the stuff of fantasy, could this be happening?

'I want you to make love to me. I want us to be close and – sexy.'

Roy didn't need any further invitation.

Some time later, impossible to say how long, Roy eased his spent body to the side of the bed and planted a warm grateful kiss on his wife's lips. She was already half-asleep, a satisfied smile on her face.

Susie found him sitting at the kitchen table with a glass of water. He looked bemused.

'G'day, Dad. Hey, are you all right?'

'Yes, yes, I'm fine. Super fine in fact!'

'What are you talking about?'

'Susie, that float or whatever it was that your mother had. It's had an effect on her.'

'What do you mean? It wasn't only the float you know. I also ordered a subliminal tape to be played to help her get over her anxiety.'

'It did more than that! Give me the phone, love. What's the number of that place?'

Susie handed him the phone and watched him dial the number. She didn't know what to think. Was he going to make a complaint?

'Hello, is that the manager? It's Roy Hawkins here. My wife attended your place today with my daughter – you weren't there, your wife was?'

Roy looked across at Susie who nodded in agreement.

'No, there's no problem. In fact just the opposite. It's had a wonderful effect on her. I still can't believe it. What I want to do is make a weekly booking for her, and that tape thing ... that's right, the same one. I'd like to have her go more often, but I don't know if I could keep up, if you know what I mean!'

He finished with a definitely lewd laugh. Susie was, by now, completely mystified.

As was Jack Campbell at the leisure centre. He had had some favourable reports from customers, but none as extravagant as this. And from Roy Hawkins, of all people.

He moved over to the hi-fi machine to check on the tape. As usual his wife hadn't put it back in its sleeve. Beth had been in Cubicle 1 according to the booking diary.

The realisation struck. Carol hadn't checked the title of the tape that had been ordered, she'd simply activated the one that was already there. A visiting football player had occupied that cubicle the day before, his choice of tape had stayed in the machine.

Enlightenment came when he read the title before returning it to its proper place. So, 'Revive your Erotic Self' really works, eh? Must try it myself, he thought. Or better still, pop it in when Carol decides to have a float. He re-examined the tape. Something niggled in the back of his mind. Sure enough, in fine print, was a warning: 'This must not be used without the agreement of the listener.' So, in a way, by playing it without Beth's knowledge, an ethical standard had been breached, a bit like the spiking of drinks leading to date rape.

I'll have to do something, he thought. This could have serious ramifications. But what? Perhaps the best thing to do would be to speak to the daughter and be guided by her opinion. He put the sign 'Back in 15' on the outer door and headed for the Hawkins place.

Roy opened the door and responded to the introduction with a hearty handshake.

'Come in, come in, I'm very pleased to meet you.'

Recognising the voice, Susie came into the living room to greet their visitor. Thinking on his feet, Jack came up with a reason for his unannounced visit.

'I try to make a point of getting feedback from anyone who's used a flotation tank for the first time. So I'm really here to talk to your wife. And also explain what happened.'

'Oh, you don't need to worry – she's very happy about it.' Roy sounded very positive.

'What do you mean "what happened"?' Susie asked sharply.

They all looked around as Beth appeared at the door.

'Mrs Hawkins? I'm Jack Campbell from the leisure centre. You met my wife when you came for a float earlier today.'

'That's right, Mr Campbell. She was very kind.'

'Yes. Well I'm here to ask you how you found your first experience, and also to explain something to you.'

Beth looked at her husband and daughter as though not sure what to say.

'I'm sorry, I've been having a little sleep, I'm not thinking very clearly. But it was something that has helped me.' She turned to Roy, a little smile on her face. 'Helped me a lot,' she said with conviction.

Tempting as it might have been to leave it at that, Jack Campbell felt obliged to admit a mistake had been made.

'The problem is, Mrs Hawkins, that the wrong tape was played in your tank. I want to apologise for that.'

'But Mum seems very relaxed after having it,' Susie put in.

'What do you mean, tape?' Beth asked. 'I only heard some vague music and the sound of waves and voices you couldn't hear. That was fine, I really liked it. In fact I'd like to do it all again, now I know what to expect.'

Roy nodded in agreement, a wide smile on his face.

'It was very thoughtful of you to come and check it out with us, but I can assure you we're all very happy.'

What more can I do? thought Jack Campbell as he left. Then a solution came into his mind. He would relabel the tape in question as 'For Beth Hawkins Only'. He'd make sure Carol knew it was to be reserved for her bookings as requested, but there was no need to explain in detail. Best keep it a secret, being well aware of the possibility of small-town gossip.

It was quite a heady feeling to know he could make everybody happy.

Never Look Back

Frobisher's voice has his characteristically smarmy tone. 'Come up and see me. I've got something you might be interested in.' It occurs to me it could almost be a come-on line. I reject it instantly. From anyone else maybe, not old Frobisher, sixty if he's a day.

When you're freelancing, as I've been for the last two years, an editor's summons has to be listened to. The *Age* hasn't given me much so far, mainly female interest stuff like current racetrack fashion or 'The Day My Youngest Started School'. All totally forgettable.

But Frobisher has moved on to the *Good Weekend*, which makes the prospect of doing something for him much more interesting. Might even be something I could get stuck into before the Big Trip Back. Funny how when I left the UK after ten years there because Dad was dying, it was also because Gerard couldn't, or more accurately, wouldn't commit. The right decision for me, absolutely. Funny, now I'm equally determined to go back. So a nice little commission would help. And perhaps my own by-line ...

The session with Frobisher takes no more than ten minutes. He greets me with his usual oily smirk, but that expression becomes serious as he gets into describing the assignment.

'It was a headline-grabbing story nearly five years ago,' he says. 'All the gruesome elements people slaver over – prison escape, abduction, murder and the perpetrator's violent death. It was front- or second-page stuff for over a week. The victim's body wasn't found for some time. Do you remember it?'

He shoves a folder containing several newspaper clippings across the table to me. Yes, the story had made the UK press. Vaguely familiar with it, I nod.

'What I'm thinking of is a survivor piece, the husband mainly. Kids if they're around. Human interest stuff five years on. Is he over it, or isn't he? New partner – marriage even? Or not? And how do the locals view it? I think there's a market for this sort of thing, people are curious. "Where was I when it happened?" Like JFK's assassination. Or Princess Di's if they're younger. That sort of thing.'

I sit for a moment, thinking. I voice my thoughts. They come out slowly.

'It would all depend on what's his name – Colin Strickland, that's it – if he agreed to retell the story and his current life, it could be worth following up.' I pause. 'Or not. I mean he might have made a recovery, a new start, might have moved away even. Do we know anything of this?' A shake of his head and an open-handed gesture towards me. I go on. 'He might not want this all brought up again.'

Frobisher is impassive. 'Yeah, of course. Well, an initial contact would establish whether we get a green light or not. Then maybe, just maybe, he might be ready to get it off his chest. Talk about it to someone outside his circle.' He's looking at me. Waiting. 'Tell you what,' he says, 'take the files, have a good look through them. See if there's any angle that might be worth exploring, then get back to me, eh?'

Before I can mouth the word 'when,' he goes on: 'Make it Monday. Then you'd need a couple of weeks to research it and write it up. That would allow us to publish it as close to the five-year anniversary as we can get. Okay? Maureen can get all the contact details for you. Also a photographer if you need one.'

I'm back on the street with the thick folder under my arm and the disconcerting realisation that I haven't discussed the financial part. Must be slipping .

Trying to make sense of the contents of the file, I spread all the bits over the table. They're not in chronological sequence. I need to get them into some sort of order to tell the story. There's a noise at the door behind me, and I sense someone come in. I don't need to second-guess – it'll be Meeg from across the corridor of the Brunswick share house, where the other three are all students of something or other. Makes one feel like an older aunt, a maiden one at that. That's ten years seniority, or more, for you.

'Wotcha up to, Jo? Feel like a coffee or something?'

Megan ('Don't call me that. Or Meg. I only answer to Meeg'), as always, fills the room with her presence. Not so much pretty as pert, sandy-haired rather than blonde, short, compact. She reminds me of the Energiser Bunny. She's immediately checking the table.

'What's all this?'

'It may be an assignment, Meeg. I'm just getting familiar with the material.'

She picks up one of the newspaper clippings with the garish headline: 'Prison escapee shot dead!' and subheading: 'Where is Linda?'

'Hey, I remember this! I was in year ten at school. Gee, it was a real live murder mystery.' She smacks her lips in excitement.

Part of me wants to gather everything up and look at it in my own good time. But an inner voice prevails – Meeg Jones' recollection might be very useful.

'I was overseas when it all happened, I'm not that clued

up on it. Why don't you tell me the story, as much as you remember. Tell it as though I know nothing about it at all.'

Meeg doesn't need persuasion. As a second-year drama student, any opportunity to take the floor is instantly accepted. She takes about twenty seconds to pace around, obviously collecting her thoughts, and launches into her monologue, making the most of any dramatic possibility.

'We need to start with Patrick Earnshaw. He's been given a long sentence, twenty years if I remember right, for the murder of his wife.

'She was going to leave him, he strangled her. He was well into his time when he was transferred to Norwood regional prison. Apparently they do the first part of a long sentence in maximum security then go to a medium security country one if their behaviour has been satisfactory. He'd been at Norwood for about eighteen months when he made his break-out. No-one seems to know what prompted that, but there was a rumour that he was told his daughter had become mixed up in the drug scene. I don't know whether that was actually true, but it is well-known that sometimes prisoners wind each other up with false information, at least that's what the teacher said.'

Her eyes are shining; she embellishes the account with hand gestures. I silently applaud her performance while registering her last phrase for future questioning.

'The prison investigation into the escape was a hush-hush affair,' she continues. 'I suppose it has to be. Can't have the general public alarmed by failures in the system or give other prisoners ideas. Afterwards there were a couple of dismissals of prison staff, so it was either negligence or corruption. That part has been kept classified apparently. Anyway, at the time, he was missing at muster and the usual alert went out, initially to the local police and then a warning broadcast through the media. So much for that part of the story. We now need to meet the Stricklands, Colin and Linda.'

She pauses and swallows. I offer her a glass of water. She declines.

'He was a High School maths teacher, in his mid-forties I think. She was an enrolled nurse working at the local hospital. Apparently it was her second marriage, his first. She had a son from her first marriage, in his twenties I suppose, lived away from home.'

She pauses in dramatic effect. 'Home is a modest weatherboard California bungalow in the outskirts of Ranfield, which is in Central Victoria, about five kilometres from Norwood Prison. Smallish town. The Stricklands were well-known and liked, especially Linda. Colin has been described as more reserved.'

She pauses for a moment and helps herself to the glass of water.

'You've got amazing recall, Meeg. And you're making the story sound so real.' I am genuinely impressed.

'It's all coming back to me.' She gives a slightly shamefaced smile. 'I guess I should admit that I picked this case to work on for my Legal Studies assignment in year eleven. Anyway, let's get down to the action part. What we know is that on this particular night in October it had been raining on and off for days. Linda came home late from work. The person doing the next shift had been held up for some reason and Colin was not pleased. Even less so when she said she had to go to a church meeting which had been called without warning. One of the articles I read said they had an argument. He didn't want her to go out again, and anyway, they hadn't had dinner. She stood her ground and asked if she could take his car. He refused and told her to take her own if she insisted on going.'

Meeg pauses, her tone changes.

'We know all this because there was an article about his feelings of guilt about that decision. You might even have that article somewhere in the pile. You see, his car was an automatic with a key locking system. Hers was a little manual hatchback with individual door locks. All this becomes crucial later on.'

By now I am completely intrigued. Another sip of water and Meeg continues.

'It seems that Linda was running late for the meeting and raced into the church hall without locking the driver's door. The hall was quite well lit but not the car park. It was a dark, rainy night, no moon at all.

'Oh, another thing Linda forgot in her haste was her mobile phone, which she left on the passenger seat. Colin Strickland rang her to apologise, but she didn't get the call.' She pauses. 'So his last words to her were never heard.'

There is an interruption. A male voice sounds outside in the corridor. 'Megan – Meeg – where the hell are you?'

She instantly becomes her normal self. 'I'm in here with Jo,' she yells. 'Be with you in a tick.' She turns to me, a look of apology on her face. 'It's Tony, I'd better go. Sorry. Can we go on with this later. It's so exciting!'

Sure, I nod. She's off out the door leaving the room palpably depleted of energy. At the same time I feel a sense of relief. I can get to read the material at my own pace. One thing's becoming obvious though – the prospect of writing up an aftermath has me intrigued.

By Sunday night I'm confident about the sequence of the events. The two stories run parallel initially: 'Prison escape – general alert. Public warned not to approach,' etc, etc. 'Local woman fails to return home after church committee meeting. Was driving a maroon Mazda hatchback. Disappearance out of character, husband very concerned,' etc, etc. Then a column making the suggestion of a link: 'Bad weather hampers the police search for prison escapee Patrick Earnshaw which is now in its second day. The public is asked to look out for a maroon Mazda sedan, registration PRZ 407, which was driven by missing Ranfield woman Linda Strickland. Police are considering a possible connection between these two events.'

I deliberately stop myself from reading later reports. Obviously, my immediate concern is to make contact with Colin Strickland. If his point of view is to be the focus of my research I need to engage with him. The neatly typed page Maureen included has names, addresses and phone numbers relevant to the case. Naturally Colin Strickland's is top of the list.

I decide to write in simple, neutral terms identifying myself as a journalist who would like to do a follow-up article about the events of nearly five years ago. Specifically, I state that I would like to identify if there were any gaps in the provision of support that might have helped. Would he be agreeable to my visit to discuss it? I finish with my phone numbers, landline and mobile. A few adjustments to the script, envelope addressed, stamped and I'm out the door to the postbox two streets away.

Making decisions and acting on them has always had a positive effect on me. I almost feel like bursting into song. Commonsense tells me he may not respond to the invitation, may refuse outright to see me and that would be that. But one lives on hope. I allow myself to think the old cliché that I would never use in my writing.

Frobisher is cordial, though a bit distracted, when I phone him on Monday to say I'd like to tackle this assignment, providing Colin Strickland agrees.

'Good,' he says. 'Thought you might. If it's a goer, you can come in, and I'll authorise enough to cover reasonable expenses.'

A pleasant flush of satisfaction suffuses me.

There are plenty of things I could/should be doing, like housework, ironing – forget it. I am inexorably drawn to the writing area of the table where I've organised all the clippings and articles into neat piles. Re-reading has made most of them familiar. I find myself approving the writing style of the main investigator, and less enamoured of the more lurid reporting in the opposition newspaper.

I'm sitting there engrossed, with my back to the open door when, suddenly, firm hands go over my eyes and mouth. My scream is smothered, I try to bite but can't. I almost can't breathe. It's blind panic. The hands are removed, and all becomes normal again. I see Meeg standing there laughing.

'What the hell do you think you're doing – you scared the shit out of me!'

'Ah, there's a purpose to it. That was one of the experiences we went through when we were studying the Linda Strickland story. We did it in pairs, one being her at the wheel of her car, the other Patrick Earnshaw emerging from the back seat. It was scary. In fact one of the kids told her parents, said she had nightmares or something and they complained to the school. And guess what – they took that case study off the syllabus. In fact, we had to hand in everything we'd already done. But it certainly made us think what it must've been like for her, poor thing.' I say nothing, but privately agree. It was a horrible experience.

'Okay, I get what you're on about. I think my heart rate's back to normal now. But you gave me a hell of a fright.' She looks minimally contrite. 'I'm sorry you had to lose all the work you'd done. But can I ask you one thing? Did you get any opportunity to put yourselves into Earnshaw's position? I mean, did he intend to kill her?'

'Some things weren't all that clear. We knew she was choked to death, but they found deep scratches on his face which probably came from her fighting him off. Perhaps she was resisting him forcing her to drive in a certain direction and he applied enough force to kill her, then realised he'd have to get rid of her so he ditched the body in that remote area where it was found. He would have heard the police helicopter, and realising there'd be road blocks, went off-road onto a bush track until he ran out of fuel. We thought he'd probably gone to sleep in the car and planned to find his way out of the bush in the daylight.'

I find the news report with the front page headline: 'Prison escapee shot dead. Where is Linda?' But Meeg doesn't need to refresh her memory. She continues with gusto.

'The car was spotted, by the helicopter searchlights, wasn't it, and police, several carloads of them, tracked him down, high-beam headlights on, and yelled through a megaphone for him to come out with his hands up. The cops, all armed, took up positions all around. The senior cop shouted for him to release Linda Strickland and to get out of the car. Eventually he did come out and staggered to his feet. He looked as though he was going to put his hands on his head when he suddenly dived over to his right between two beams of headlights. One of the cops shouted, 'Stop or I'll fire!' He doesn't stop. Later, they said they aimed at his knees but he slipped and fell in the damp undergrowth. One of the shots was fatal, right in the chest.' Meeg pauses for breath.

'I know, I've read up on the next bit. They find Linda is not in the car. And the abductor's dead. It becomes a grim mystery, with no real clues as to her whereabouts. They checked the mileage on the car to try to calculate how far he'd travelled. Soil analysis of the tyres. Urgent calls for sightings and so on. I guess everyone was hoping she'd managed to escape. But that wasn't the case, as things turned out.'

We're both silent for a few moments. I snap out of it. 'Let's have a drink, this has all been a bit heavy. And remember, nothing might come of it anyway.'

She smiles and takes the stubby of Fosters offered.

Two days later I get a phone call from Colin Strickland. Polite. Dull voice. But an acceptance, that was the main thing. Yes he would be glad to talk to me. Any time. Gave his telephone number as well.

Yippee! I squeal after putting the phone down. This could be a very worthwhile assignment. Already I'm visualising the banner headline: 'Five Years On. A soul-searching account of one man's journey through unimaginable loss. An exclusive by Joanne Warner ....'

It's been five days since I arrived in Ranfield. Time to make a decision. Is there enough to draft into a story. I have to be honest, the pickings are slim. Nothing new, really. Five years after the tragedy, people still want to talk about it, as you'd expect. I go through the list of contacts and it all pans out the same, though with some variation according to an individual's take on it. 'If only' features a lot. If only Earnshaw hadn't made a successful escape from prison on that night, if only the church meeting had been held a week later when it was supposed to be, if only Colin had cooperated and let her take his Toyota Camry with its central locking system. 'No-one round here worries too much about locking car doors, but when it's just a click on a key holder, you do it automatically,' someone said.

The minister of the church Linda attended had clearly reached out to Colin in his bereavement but had been rebuffed. 'He seems to think we were in some way responsible for Linda being where she was that night. We pray for him of course, but he's put up barriers against us.' Everyone said the same thing, more or less. All overtures were resisted.

Colin Strickland took early retirement on medical grounds and retreated into his own world. After five years, nothing had changed.

In the drab little hotel room, I scan the handwritten notes. The effect of elapsed time on the nearest relative – that would have been the main thrust of my article. And there hasn't been anything new in what I've gleaned from talking with Colin. Everything so far has been – it sounds cruel to say it – predictable. He's hanging on to the anger and guilt. Hasn't moved on, to use the phrase in current use, or more correctly, overuse. It's obvious people have tried to help him, he says so himself. But he can't. Or won't.

So what can I work with here? It's morbidly fascinating in a way, but would the headline: 'Five Years On – and the Pain Remains' really grab a reader's interest? I think not. I could do with the money, that's a given, but ...

Decision time. I'll ring Frobisher tomorrow and tell him. Today will be my last foray into Colin Strickland's miserable, static world.

He opens the door some thirty seconds after I ring the bell. His appearance seems unchanged, shoulders still slumped. His eyes flicker over me briefly before he lowers his gaze and motions me inside. It's mid-afternoon but the curtains are drawn, as they have been on my previous visits. I try to rehearse in my mind what I want to say to him.

Basically that this will be goodbye and its very likely nothing will come from my visit here.

He surprises me with his next words.

'I'm glad you've come. I've been thinking. You know when you wrote that letter saying you wanted to find out how I could have been helped more at the time.'

'Ah – yes, I did. Have you thought of something that has been overlooked?'

'Yes. Well, yes, and no. It's not so much at the time as – all the time. Can you help me?'

'I could try, of course, if you could tell me what it's about.'

We move to the two armchairs where we've sat previously. This time he remains standing. I wonder what's on his mind. He slowly turns to face me, then seems to address the back wall.

'Have you heard of PTSD ?'

'Post Traumatic Stress Disorder? I have heard of it.'

'There was an article about it in one of Linda's old magazines. I was going to throw them out when the title of one of the articles seemed to speak to me. It was called 'The Enemy Within'. It was about soldiers being tormented by memories of things they'd witnessed on active duty. It was for them like it is for me: flashbacks, intrusive pictures that come the minute you close your eyes, the horror of it all.' His voice is intense, his breathing's quickened.

I consider carefully how to respond. 'Is this something you should tell your doctor? Or a counsellor?'

'No.' His voice is emphatic. 'No. I did see Dr Young straight after it – it happened. He got me an appointment with a lady psychiatrist, I can't remember her name. She just went on about the grieving process and told me it was all normal, though painful, and gave me tablets which made me feel like a zombie but probably kept me from ending it all. No, those horrible, disgusting revolting things didn't surface then, not like they are now.'

I'm a bit stuck here. I decide to try a factual approach as far as I can. 'My understanding of PTSD is that it is a consequence of something a person has seen, or did, or happened to them. In your situation – although you suffered a terrible loss ...'

He interrupts me roughly. 'But that's just it! It IS what I saw – that's what's tormenting me. I can't stop seeing it and thinking of it all the time ...'

His voice is loud and insistent. I feel a bit nervous. Is there an aspect to this story I know nothing about? 'Could you, can you tell me what it is exactly that distresses you so much?'

'I'm going to try and tell you, if you'll listen. No-one really listened to me when I tried to explain what happened. Whenever I tried to describe it, the attitude was that it was all in my mind, an hallucination, not real. Believe me, Joanne, this is real!'

The intensity behind his words grips me. I have to hear him out, even though there seems to be a hint of madness there.

'Colin – could you start at the beginning and just talk quietly through it and I'll listen, I promise.'

'Thank you.' He sounds relieved and sits down on the edge of the seat of the armchair facing me. 'I'll start back when they found Linda's body. Do you remember how that happened? It was reported on, just like everything else.'

I search my memory. 'Wasn't it a farmer ...?'

'Yes, a farmer noticed several crows in a scrubby corner of one of his paddocks not far from that dirt road. He thought it must have been one of his sheep down. Crows always circle a stricken animal. They go for the eyes.' He gulps at this and takes a moment to compose himself. 'It was Linda's body. It had been there for over a week. It all happened quickly after that – the police, the ambulance, then the mortuary at the Base Hospital. The detective in charge of the case, Bob Cutmore his name was, rang me. I'll never forget his words. 'Colin,' he said. 'We think we've found Linda. We need you for the identification. Sorry to have to tell you like this.' He came round and drove me to the hospital morgue.' He pauses.

'But before we could go in, one of the attendants came out in a hurry to have a private word with him. "Colin," Bob asked, "we need to know what colour your wife's eyes were." I said, "She has brown eyes." The attendant nodded and left.

Some five minutes later we were ushered in. I was given a mask to wear, so was Bob. To minimise the stench, I realised later. I remember looking at the body lying there on the table. It was Linda. They only showed her head which was all that was needed to confirm the identity. Her face was familiar, but all mottled and blotchy, a blue-grey colour. The rest was covered by a heavy off-white sheet. "It's Linda," I said. It was incredible that I could say anything at all. I felt totally numb, shocked, a bit nauseous. "Thank you, Colin. We needed to be sure, of course," said Bob at the door, indicating for us to leave.'

He takes the smallest of pauses before continuing.

'I should have gone straight out. I didn't. I turned back for one last look at my dead wife in time to see the attendant gouging out an eyeball, leaving a gaping black hole. And coming out of that hole was a maggot, slowed because of the chilling, but a live crawling maggot. There may have been more but that's the one I saw. That's what I saw then, and that's what I see now. Every night and often through the day. I can't control it, the image just comes – and I know my wife's brain was teeming with maggots eating it away ... it's hideous, it's horrible. I can't make it go away. Nothing makes that image leave my mind.'

His face is white, he looks spent. He lowers himself down into the chair. In a flash of insight I understand why there aren't any photos of Linda on display, except for one where she's laughing with her head thrown back. He's next to her in the large framed snapshot, a smile on his face.

For perhaps the first time he looks directly at me. 'Your eyes are brown too. Just like Linda's.'

His observation has a paralysing effect on me. I struggle to find the right words. To thank him for confiding in me, to say I wouldn't be writing an article for the *Age*. Whatever way I might put it sounds so lame. Most of all, I want to get out, to go, go as far as possible from that awful picture he's described, which is now not only in his tortured mind but also in mine.

That is my immediate reaction. I hold onto it for what seems to be an age.

Then I become aware of Colin's eyes staring, the gaze intense, desperate, beseeching ... help me, please help me.

I feel myself drawn to him in a way that's absolutely different to anything I've ever felt before. I want to help him. I have an irresistible impulse to gather him in my arms to comfort him. He doesn't expect this, he's tense against my embrace. Then, with a shuddering sigh, as though all the breath he's been holding onto is expelled, he slumps on my shoulder as I kneel before him.

I feel incredibly powerful. A Mother Earth feeling. I murmur something inane like 'It's all right, it's all right.' I gently pat his back, much as you would soothe a child.

My mind's quick, always has been. Typical Gemini. But never as fast as it's racing now. Somehow, in this most bizarre of circumstances, a connection has been made that is so profound, so meaningful, that I know nothing will ever be the same again. It's like one of those mind-blowing epiphanies, like being in mortal danger and your whole life flashes in front of you. Or so they say. What I'm seeing now – suddenly uninviting – is the prospect of returning to the UK and trying again with Gerard. Or if that fails, putting myself out in the singles scene again ...

Or ... Or looking at the situation here, right here and now. This man, with his tragic story, trusts me. And I respond to his neediness. I recognise that: a need to be needed. Together we could explore resources that might help him. I could research about the condition, find out what's available, be there to support him, share the painful steps to recovery, whatever's necessary. Encourage him to start living again, be a companion, a confidante, or more ....

I would have a role to play, and a future. That sense of deep emptiness I've been feeling for so long is dissipating. I look at him, smiling. Can't help it.

Without the faintest idea of what's been going through my mind, he manages a lop-sided sort of smile in reply.

SHOVE OFF

How do you get rid of someone? I don't mean shooting or poisoning or anything illegal like that. When hints, then requests and, finally, demands, don't work it can all seem pretty hopeless. But it can be done. And the truth is you don't have to be nasty to anyone who's well and truly outlived his welcome. In fact – just the opposite.

A few years ago, Mum had inherited the house in Newstead after her parents died, so we moved up from Melbourne. Marion was going to the High School in Castlemaine and I'd just started prep at the local primary school. Even Mum and Dad were getting on all right then, though Mum seemed to be the one who had to worry about not having enough money. Dad was a bit of a gambler and usually a loser. Mum was like her Methodist parents and dead against it. 'Even if you win,' she'd say, 'It's tainted money and I don't want a bar of it.'

They used to argue about Dad's work, or lack of it, 'Well you wanted to come up here to live, Dell. I always managed to get a few jobs when we lived in Footscray. There just isn't anything goin' around here.' Then Mum would have her say: 'You could've got a job at that factory where Lloyd works and come home here at weekends.'

Dad's expression said it all. He didn't like Mum's brother. We didn't either.

The last time my uncle came up was during his annual

leave a year or so ago. I was twelve at the time and going to High School, while Marion had left school and was working in a cafe in Castlemaine to save money as she wanted to do a course at uni in Melbourne.

It turned out his marriage was pretty rocky. Not really surprising given that Uncle Lloyd always seemed to say the sort of thing that turned people against him. Like when I walked down the main street of Castlemaine with him and we came across Cheryl Twycross, one of the Newstead girls who left school early, sitting with some of her friends outside one of the coffee shops yakking. She was giving her baby a bottle of milk. Uncle Lloyd looked her up and down and said: 'What's up with your tits? Don't they work?' That stirred the pigeons, I can tell you.

Even though Dad had been away working on trawlers in the Northern Territory for quite a while, Uncle Lloyd used to bad-mouth him at the dinner table. When Marion tried to stick up for Dad, he said: 'Your mother wouldn't 'ave looked twice at him if she hadn't been up the duff with you.' That made Mum really cross. 'How do you know what I would or wouldn't do. Anyway we went on to have another child, so what does that tell you?'

'That you were careless!' He laughed that horrible sniggering laugh of his. Marion and I left the table before we'd even finished.

'If you want to go back tomorrow I'll drive you to the station,' Mum said. He pulled his head in after that, but it annoyed me that he didn't do anything round the place to help Mum. As the man of the house now, I still had to chop the wood and feed the chooks.

Anyway, he finally left, and a few of the neighbours had a word with Mum afterwards. I overheard Betty Irving apologise for not visiting. She said: 'I can't stomach that brother of yours,

Dell. He gives me the creeps.' He'd said some funny things to me too, like: 'Are you up to beatin' the meat yet?' When I asked Mum what he meant she'd had a real go at him.

We settled down to our routine again. Marion got herself into the welfare course she wanted to do at uni, and Dad sent a bit of money through to the bank to help keep us going. I really missed him, though I got to talk on the phone a few times, about every two months, but when he was out to sea he couldn't even send us letters. He wasn't much for writing anyway. Now I'm in my second year at high school catching the bus like Marion did, and Mum's been doing a bit of part-time work in the old people's ward at the hospital. She hasn't got proper qualifications, only a sort of TAFE course, but she likes it.

The big news was about old Tucker's place which is down the road from us. It had been empty for years and was really run-down when, guess what? Two women and a little kid moved in. They came on a Saturday in an old Ford ute with a sort of canopy on the back where you could see bits of furniture poking out. Mum and I were both home and could see what was going on,

'They don't seem to have any men to help them,' she commented. Then, 'Would you like to go over and offer yourself?' I didn't mind. You couldn't expect old Jack Howard, their next-door neighbour, to get involved. He was probably ninety.

Anyway, they were friendly and grateful for my help, not that I did much. The inside of the house was incredibly dusty and needed a good clean-up. Janie, the younger one, who seemed to laugh a lot, suggested they should clean out one room first and put their belongings in there. The other one, whose name was Sandra, was bigger and stronger. She got busy with the broom and dustpan. She and I did most of the heavy work lifting the furniture off the back of the ute. We were lifting an old couch together when I felt something hit my legs. 'Oh, Beppi, you little devil – come here out of the way. You could have done Billy some damage.' That was Janie's voice. To my surprise I heard a little kid's yell – I'd thought Beppi was a dog!

They offered me a coke after we'd got everything inside and we could take a breather. Then I asked: 'Who's Beppi's Mum?' They looked at each other and then back at me. 'We both are.' I must have looked a bit confused 'cos Sandra went on to say: 'He hasn't got a dad, he's just got us. We're his family.' I got a look at the little fellow. He looked about one to me, not that I'm an expert or anything. He could walk, with a waddle, and talk a bit. He was cute with curly blonde hair. He looked a happy little fellow.

Mum was a bit subdued when I repeated what I'd been told about the newcomers. 'We'll just have to see whether they'll be made welcome.'

In time, they did seem to fit in all right. They got involved with local things like the community garden, the op-shop and the childminding centre. I suppose there are a few other single-parent families around. Someone said it was easier to manage on benefits in the country. Personally, I think it's a much better place to bring up kids.

Then one day, Mum got a phone call from Lloyd. She told me about it later, she was almost apologetic. 'Look, Billy, I couldn't really refuse. He is family.' When I asked what she was on about, she said: 'He's had an accident and can't work. But the accident didn't happen at work, so he can't get workers' comp.' She paused, then the punchline came. 'Shirley's kicked him out and he has nowhere to live. So what could I say?'

'He's coming here?'

'Yes.'

'For how long?' Mum just shook her head.

When I heard the car pull up and heard two doors shut, I braced myself for what I knew would be his words of greeting. 'Well hello, Billy. Still little Billy, I see.' That was below the belt. I was very conscious that I wasn't even as tall as Mum, who's pretty average. I kept hoping I was a late starter and would shoot up overnight. But it hadn't happened yet.

'Hello, Uncle Lloyd. Sorry to hear you've had an accident. What happened?'

For answer he stuck out his foot. The left one was enclosed in a big sort of slipper. I noticed he was using a walking stick.

He took over Marion's room and proceeded to make it into a pigsty. He insisted on smoking inside, in spite of Mum's disapproval. 'It's for me nerves,' he said. 'I've been through a lot, you know.' Apparently the accident happened when he stepped against the lights into the path of an oncoming car.

'Sorry I won't be able to help much, Dell,' he said. As if he ever did, I thought.

It took a few days for him to notice that someone was living in Tucker's place. The smoke coming from the chimney was pretty much a giveaway.

'So who's livin' over there?' When we told him, his immediate response was: 'Lessos? Lessos here? God help us!' '

'They're all right, Lloyd. They've fitted into the community okay.'

'I can't stand them. It's – it's unnatural. Bet the old timers round here don't approve.'

Whether they did or not I don't know, but nothing was ever said. Except by Lloyd. He resumed his old habit of a six o'clock visit to the pub. 'Lucky it's within walking distance,' he said. Mum wasn't so pleased. 'You never know when he's coming back for dinner.'

Several times she got a phone call from the publican for her to pick him up. 'A few too many, Dell. And he's got quite mouthy.'

43

When sober, Lloyd wasn't noted for his charm. But when he had a bit of grog in him, nothing escaped his critical analysis: the government, the immigrants, and closer to home, same-sex partnerships. It was this which got him into most trouble. It seems that Sandra and Janie had become accepted in the community, and his comments about their relationship were not well received at all.

Sometimes Lloyd would broach the subject of Mum's inheritance of the property. I didn't know all that much about this, but, head bent over my homework, I overheard the argument that always followed. 'You decided to take the money and I had the house. That was agreed.'

'That was Shirley's idea. She didn't want to live in the country. Maybe I should have stuck out for a half-share.'

'Well, you didn't. There's no point in going on about it.'

So it was a sort of uneasy truce for the next few months until the fire. In a way, it was just as well Lloyd was out of town when it happened or he might have come under suspicion, since his attitude to the lesbian couple was so well-known. As it happened, he had an appointment to see the orthopaedic surgeon at the Alfred, so he caught the early train to Melbourne. Mum dropped him off at the station before she went to work.

'He managed to cadge a bed at an old mate's place so he'll stay down for a few days,' she told me later.

'I wish it was for a few months,' I muttered.

Mum heard me, but didn't say anything. The look on her face said it all.

The fire – yes, the fire. It was pretty awful and could have been worse, especially for little Beppi. The local news report said a log rolled out of the fireplace and set fire to the carpet and furniture. Being an old timber house it spread quickly.

Apparently, Beppi had climbed out of his cot and trotted over to the big urn they had attached by a hook to the big iron bar across the open fireplace. He must have reached through the fire-screen and turned on the tap, letting all the water out. Then the heat of the blazing fire caused the urn to explode. Sandra and Janie were outside. They heard the noise, rushed inside to find Beppi screaming with pain from the scalding and gasping in the smoke and steam. They covered him in a sheet and rang for an ambulance, the police and the fire brigade. The main worry was the little boy – both of them went in the emergency ambulance to the Bendigo hospital, sirens screaming.

The fire brigade couldn't save the house, the flames had taken hold, and at the end of the day only a charred shell remained. They had lost everything. It made the TV news and the papers, of course. The main concern was for the little boy. There was relief all around when the bulletins from the hospital were positive. He was going to live. Even the scalded areas weren't as extensive as first thought. A few local people visited the hospital to offer support, and to find out what Janie and Sandra wanted to do. Mum said to me they could've stayed with us if Lloyd wasn't there.

Sure enough, he turned up six days later, all agog. 'Bit of excitement in the bush, eh? I suppose it's one way to get rid of them.'

'What are you talking about? They're not going anywhere. They want to stay here, they're definite about that. And there's been two community meetings in the hall – everybody wants to help. They've started a fund, and we're looking into getting another house for them.'

Lloyd was not impressed. He continued with snide comments such as: 'I suppose they weren't insured, were they.' To which Mum replied: 'Are you?' which shut him up.

He resisted any invitation to join in fundraising, even though his medical report showed good recovery from his injury. He hadn't shown it to us, choosing to deny there was any improvement. Mum found it under his bed. She noted the report finished by advising exercise and activity to strengthen his leg. When she asked whether he was ready to go back to work, perhaps on light duties, he refused to consider it, saying he needed more time.

I felt sorry for Mum. We hadn't heard from Dad for quite a while, which meant there wasn't any money coming in from him. It wasn't until I heard her on the phone talking to Marion that I realised she was getting desperate. She motioned me over. It was good to talk to my sister, I really missed her. 'What do you think's the worst thing that's happening for Mum?' she asked. I looked around. Lloyd was down at the pub again. I could speak freely.

'What's getting her down most is having Uncle Lloyd here. He's so negative about everything, especially about the fire. Everyone else's trying to help except him. And he won't go. I'm sick of him too.' Marion assured me that she would give it some thought. She promised to come up for a visit at the end of the semester. That would be good, even if I had to give up my room and sleep on the couch.

The fundraising for Sandra and Janie was going along slowly. They had found another house to rent, but needed absolutely everything to furnish it. People donated stuff, like they always do when there's an emergency like a flood or bushfire. Little Beppi was still in hospital, so they would take it in turns to drive up in the ute to be with him. The one not at the hospital was often invited to an evening meal with one or other family. I knew Mum would have liked to be part of this too, but Lloyd could not be trusted to be friendly. Instead, she sometimes took a casserole to their new house.

The community ran sausage sizzles in Castlemaine, a garage sale or two around town and a few raffles, all in aid of the couple. I helped as much as I could. The amounts raised didn't come to much, especially as petrol costs ate into it. It was all such a struggle for them. But tired, brave smiles showed their gratitude for the help of the people of Newstead. 'We wouldn't have got this in Melbourne,' Janie said.

The phone call from Marion several weeks later was really special. I answered it, as Mum was at work and I had a study day off school. Her voice was excited, it seemed to crackle down the phone line.

'I'm coming up on Friday,' she said. 'I've got a brilliant plan! If it works it'll solve our problems, Mum's anyway. Don't say anything, though. It's success relies on secrecy.'

To say I was intrigued would be an understatement.

It was great to see her again, she looked really smart and upmarket. Mum brightened up, too, having her around. I was curious to see how Uncle Lloyd would react. He decided to criticise her uni course. 'What's the point in wasting time tryin' to help no-hopers? You'll never make any money givin' 'em handouts, won't get no thanks, either.'

'You're wrong about that, Uncle Lloyd.' I was interested to see whether she'd keep the uncle bit, given that she was twenty now. But he didn't invite her to drop it.

Over dinner, she brought up the subject of the fire at Tucker's place and asked Mum what was happening. Mum explained that the community was, with few exceptions – she looked at Lloyd – doing all they could to help resettle the women. Lloyd snorted and said that they knew what he thought about it, so he wasn't saying anything.

'Who's in charge of the fundraising?' Marion asked.

'The local copper's the main one. They've got a big chart up in the grocer's window showing how much has been raised so far. It's creeping up slowly. So far it's just over two hundred dollars, but they need a lot more than that.' Marion didn't say anything. I noticed a bit of a smile on her face.

The next day, being Saturday, Marion and I walked down the main street of Newstead. Quite a lot of people said hello to her, and introduced her to the occasional newcomer in town. She looked at the poster with its blazing red title 'FIRE APPEAL' in Pete Calligan's window and remarked on the photo of Beppi at the top. Someone had taken it when he was in hospital. He looked so little and cute with all those white bandages and a tiny smile. I suppose all their other photos had been destroyed in the fire.

'Isn't he sweet! Poor little lamb, hope he makes it all right.' She turned to me and said: 'We need to talk privately, Billy. I need your help in this, but you'll be the only one who knows. Up for it?'

'Sure.' I said, full of curiosity. We found an empty seat half-way down the street and sat down to talk.

'Do you remember telling me that the best thing that could happen for Mum would be for Lloyd to leave?' I nodded. 'That's still the case?' I nodded again. Emphatically.

She leaned towards me and whispered: 'I've got two thousand dollars in cash here.' I gasped – what was this? 'It's from Dad. He had a big win for a change. He sent it to me via my bank account and said it was for Mum, to give her what she really wanted most.'

I admit I was puzzled. 'Are you planning to pay him to go?'

'No. What I'm going to do is to give the money to the Fire Appeal.' I gasped again – all these surprises. 'It will be donated anonymously but ... let's go, you'll see.'

We headed to the policeman's home, which was the back part of the station. Colin McMaster had been our policeman for ages. His kids went to the local school, the boy, was a year below Marion and his daughter was a couple of grades ahead of me. I sometimes sat next to her on the school bus, she was okay.

'Well, hello Marion! Nice to see you, come on in, both of you.'

After a bit of preliminary chat about her welfare diploma course and asking what his son was doing, Marion came to the point.

'Mum tells me you're in charge of the fundraising for the Fire Appeal,' she said. 'It's a great thing you're all doing, I've told the staff and other students in my course about it – they're most impressed. Now I've got a big sum of money here to donate to it, but the donor definitely doesn't want to be recognised. You'd have to put it in as "Anonymous".' I was a bit confused by all this – was Dad behind it?

Senior Constable McMaster looked quite solemn. 'It's good to have any donation, of course. But if you say it's a lot of money, and we don't know who it's from, I have a bit of a problem. It could be proceeds of crime, or stolen – do you see what I'm getting at?'

I could see Marion was a bit rattled. Then she made a decision. 'Right, Mr McMaster, I'll tell you who it's from, as long as there's no publicity attached. This person couldn't handle it.'

'I take your point. And this person, between you and me, is?

'My Uncle Lloyd.'

Clearly this was the last name Mr McMaster expected to hear. He almost spluttered. 'Lloyd Parkinson? You don't say! How much is he giving?'

'Two thousand dollars.'

Colin McMaster spluttered again. 'I – almost – don't believe it!'

Marion was busy counting out the hundred dollar notes, twenty of them. I'd never seen so much money in my life, it was mesmerising. The policeman recovered his composure and, after recounting the wad of notes, separated them with rubber bands and put them in the safe. He got out the invoice book and wrote out the amount, the purpose of it, and the donor. In this space he put 'Anonymous' and 'per Marion.' He gave the receipt to her and locked the safe.

'We've got another meeting tomorrow afternoon in the community centre. I'll be able to announce a huge lift to the total. It'll give everyone a real thrill.'

'Best not mention me in that, people might guess,' Marion said.

'It's hard to imagine anyone guessing the real identity, eh, Billy?'

I had to agree. The least likely person by far. Everybody knew about his prejudices – he had not made any secret of them.

On the way home I quizzed Marion. The point of this was not at all clear to me.

'It's a bit of a gamble, Billy. But, if it works ... well, there could be two outcomes. We'll just have to wait and see. Hey, let's go along tomorrow and see people's reaction to the donation.'

Marion was right. The response to the announcement was total excitement. A buzz went round the group of thirty or so who'd come along. Janie was there, she'd given Sandra's apologies, as the older woman was doing the hospital visit.

'I can't believe it that anyone could be so generous,' she said half-smiling, half-crying to the friends who crowded around her. People kept asking Colin McMaster to give just a hint, a small clue, anything to follow up, he just smiled and shook his head. Then, relenting, he said: 'It's probably the last person you'd imagine.' That sent them buzzing again. I heard various names mentioned, but not Lloyd's. That would have been totally unbelievable.

The subject came up at dinner that night, which was only to be expected. Mum was mystified. 'It's just wonderful that someone cares enough to give that much money. I wonder who it is?'

Lloyd put his bit in. 'Some fool who's a sucker for a sob story, that's who.'

Marion said nothing. I kept my mouth shut too. I still couldn't work out the purpose of the deception. All Marion had said was: 'Trust me.' Guess I had to.

For a week or so, nothing much changed. Then it happened. A rumour started around town. Someone stopped me in the street and said: 'Who'd have thought it!' I said, 'Thought what?' 'That it was your uncle who gave all that money – didn't you know either?'

Next thing, Mum's buttonholed me. 'Do you know anything about this rumour?' Normally I would never lie, it's not worth the hassle has been my experience. This time I just put on a puzzled face and spread out my hands, palm up like they do in the movies.

Naturally, she confronted Lloyd, in a kind voice, of course. He absolutely and totally denied it. 'Everyone's convinced it's you,' she said, 'If you're just being coy about it – there's no need. People want to express their appreciation.'

Mum let Marion know of this surprising development. After a few unsuccessful attempts to reach her she finally got through. I could only hear her side of the conversation as she explained that the secret major donor had turned out to be her uncle. She went on to say he was not admitting to it, in fact was getting quite angry about all the fuss. 'Yes,' I heard her say, 'people are treating him differently but he's still denying having anything to do with it.'

'What did Marion say, Mum?'

'She seemed amazed, but really pleased that he's got a

better image in the community. She went on about self-esteem and all those social worky words, but to be honest, I can't see him enjoying being in favour for once.'

I was curious to find out how his name had been made public. Only Marion, Colin McMaster and I knew. I made it my business to sit next to Heidi McMaster on the bus and broached the subject. 'How did people find out about my uncle, do you know?'

'I think it was when Mum said to Dad the most unlikely person would have to be Dell Simpson's brother. Dad didn't say anything, he just smiled, and so she guessed. Then she told a few of her friends and word got around.' She laughed. 'It's all been such a mini-mystery, I'm going to write an essay about it for English Expression, and call it 'Local Philanthropy with a Twist'.

Her story explained it. Technically the policeman hadn't revealed the name, but he didn't refute it either.

Things were brought to a head, partly by the write-up in the local newsletter, which gave a lot of space to the fundraising campaign, with a final comment that 'a wonderful boost has come from a donor who says he wants to remain anonymous, but we suspect his initials may well be L.P. Someone who hides his heart of gold under a gruff exterior!'

Then, little Beppi was ready to be discharged from hospital. The bad news was that the old ute had broken down. The good news was that they could buy a good secondhand car from the fire fund thanks to the benefactor. Tony from the garage helped them find a neat little Nissan hatchback. Sandra and Janie were ecstatic.

The whole town seemed to share in the little fellow's homecoming, even though he was too young to understand. Mum made scones and cakes for the celebration afternoon tea they arranged in the community hall a couple of days later.

'Billy,' she said to me, a slight frown on her face, 'Sandra and Janie want to publicly thank Lloyd at this do. Do you think you could persuade him he should go and let them do this? I'll help by ironing a decent shirt and getting him smartened up, there's bound to be a photographer there.'

When I finally pinned him down, he was in a foul mood.

'I'm sick of bloody stupid women comin' up and wantin' to shake my hand. And even tryin' to kiss me,' he said, disgust written all over his face. 'I keep tellin' them I don't know nothin' about it and I don't know how this stupid rumour started, but they just smile in that soppy way. I can't stand it, I tell you. "Under it all, you're a good man," one of them said. I tell them: "Rubbish, you've got it wrong, you idiot. Leave me alone!" But they don't.'

'Maybe after the function on Thursday afternoon they'll ease up. Mum asked me to tell you they want to make a little presentation to you. Sandra and Janie really want to thank you in person. And little Beppi will be there. So – can you go through with it?'

He looked at me with what can only be described as fear in his eyes. It reminded me of the trapped wild dog I'd seen once. Desperate is probably the word.

'I've got to get out of here. What time does the bus go through? Too late for today, I'll get it tomorrow morning.'

And that's how it all ended. He threw his things together and left. His parting words were: 'I'm never comin' back to this sick community. You're all nut cases.'

Mum and I couldn't stop smiling. She gave me an enormous hug and it seemed like years dropped off her, if that makes sense. 'This is better than winning the lottery, if I believed in that sort of thing!' she said. I hinted that Marion might be able to shed some light on what happened. But I wasn't about to spill the beans. As it was, we just relished the relief of his departure.

And as for me – I'd actually grown two inches taller!

DRAW WHAT YOU SEE

Tuesday morning. Second day of the week, unless you count Sunday as the start, as some calendars do. Peter struggled to put Tuesday in the forefront of his mind. Oh yes, art class. Life drawing, to be precise.

Not his idea, art hadn't ever been his thing. But the shrink had encouraged it as something to concentrate on. Apparently he'd done a few of these courses himself in the past. 'You're depressed, you're not mad, you're –' Peter almost heard the word 'just' added, but be wisely rejected – '... as I said, depressed.' Yeah, spot on. 'We can help you with medication,' he paused. 'But you need to give yourself permission to recover.'

Huh!

Peter had disciplined himself to block out the horrific memories. He'd managed to present an intact self at the funeral, the inquest and to commiserating family and friends. Managed to keep it up for over three months until people gradually dropped off, respecting his almost apologetic request to want to deal with his loss on his own.

Then he had crashed.

Not like Linda did in an out of control car on a treacherous unmade country road. No. It had been insidious, seductive – deliberate isolation, maudlin introspection, fuelled by alcohol – leading inexorably to the sinkhole of certainty that he didn't want to live any more.

He forced himself to focus. Tuesday: art class. Actually the first four sessions hadn't been too bad. He had worried that seeing, and trying to draw, an undressed female person might be painful, but that hadn't been the case at all.

The detachment of the other students had steadied him, he realised, and, rather surprisingly, he became quite absorbed in developing latent drawing skills.

Today he considered taking a new step by trying a bit of colour. He had noted the interesting effects others achieved using watercolour or oil paint. He added the new box of pastels to his carry-all. Hopefully they were the right things to buy, they looked just like crayons kids used.

A routine check of the sky outside. Yes, it looked like rain. Take an umbrella.

In his last session with the psychiatrist, Dr Roberts had asked him to describe how he was feeling. He'd thought hard to explain his mood, but managed to come out with just two words: 'hollow' and 'heavy.' The psych didn't comment. Just keep going.

Peter nodded to the other class members. They were a mixed lot, both in appearance and talent. A few were youngish, but the majority seemed to be older men and women, probably retired. Like him.

Last week, one of the chaps had tried to be friendly. Noting Peter's wedding ring he'd said: 'wife happy about you coming here, eh?'

Peter had replied: 'my wife died in a car accident eight months ago.'

The old chap had murmured, 'Sorry,' adding with perhaps a trace of hope, 'any children?'

'We decided early on against having children.'

End of conversational exchange. So what. He didn't need to go into the heartbreak of the cancer diagnosis and subsequent hysterectomy in the early months of their marriage. It seemed to bring them closer together in the ensuing years. Until now.

Peter set up the easel and drawing board, attaching the first sheet of paper with masking tape. He was vaguely aware of today's model arriving and going straight into the curtained-off change area. The tutor busied himself preparing the small stage.

The routine was the same each week. Three five-minute poses, a break followed by two of ten minutes, another short break with a fifteen minute session leading into the main break allowing for a coffee and cigarette, for those still following the habit. After that, the long pose was set to allow the students to spend more time to develop their drawing or painting skills in the second hour of the class.

Ten o'clock. The room was comfortably full now, with the twelve or so spread around in a semi-circle. The model came out of the change room, stepped onto the platform and took off her worn robe to reveal a well-shaped body.

'Right, everyone. Three quick sketches, five minutes each,' the tutor announced.

From his position on the side, Peter had a complete back view which was satisfying to draw. Standing poses usually are, he'd decided. The next brought her face into profile. Standing again, but one hand on the back of a chair. The third brought her round to face him in full frontal exposure, and with it, a shock.

Casting his eye over the body standing motionless not more than two metres away from him, he recognised the discolouration on the inner, upper area of her left thigh – it was a bruise. It looked as though she had tried to camouflage it with flesh-coloured make-up, but the bluish tinge showed through.

His eyes went to her face and another flash of identification.

Again, there appeared to be an attempt at concealment, but there was no doubt in Peter's mind that she had a black right eye. There was momentary eye contact before her gaze lowered.

He looked around the room. Everybody seemed to be concentrating on the job in hand, though he noticed two of the women whispering. The tutor was making his rounds, checking on progress. Peter started the new drawing, but less confidently. The five-minute buzzer sounded just as the tutor appeared at his elbow.

'Okay, ten minute break.'

The model quickly gathered her robe around her body and withdrew. Peter turned to the younger man. 'Is she – all right? She seems to have, um, been in an accident or something.'

'I know. Look, she insists she's fine to model for us today. Didn't want to talk about it at all.' In a lower voice he added, 'I think she needs the money.'

The buzzer intruded again. This time the tutor had placed a chair in the middle of the small stage. The model emerged again, carefully stepped up and disrobed, allowing the gown to cover the seat. Peter noted her slight grimace as she lowered herself into a sitting position and settled into the pose.

His years as a police officer had made him sensitive to facial expressions and body language. The old familiar recording diagram flashed into his mind. Stop it, Peter. You're a civilian now, an ageing, depressed, would-be art student going through the motions of distraction therapy.

He picked up a stick of carbon and began to mark in the dimensions on the new sheet of paper. Basically a triangle shape, he decided.

The class was quiet, absorbed. Quick sketching had given way to more considered drawing, each student looking up from time to time to confirm the image being created. The tutor made his way around, occasionally taking over a student's seat and with a few expert strokes, correcting the drawing. The model kept her gaze fixed on the upper corner of the room, but as the minutes ticked by, Peter observed that her breathing was becoming a little faster and rather tense. At the sound of the buzzer, she got up abruptly, draped the gown around her and hastily re-entered the cubicle.

'All right, folks. We'll skip the next shorter pose and take the twenty-minute break now. Let's be back by eleven-fifteen for the long one.'

Usually, in the other sessions he'd attended, the model would cover herself for warmth and modesty, and wander around to see the work that had been done, often making an approving comment. This one, however, remained hidden.

As he made his way to the coffee shop, Peter asked one of the women whether they'd had this model before.

'No, not since I've been coming, and that's about two years now. She looks a bit, well, beaten-up, doesn't she, poor thing. Probably didn't feel like doing it today, but didn't want to let the tutor down.'

'Or perhaps she really needs the money,' Peter replied.

Back in the art studio, Peter saw that the tutor had placed a recliner diagonally across the stage and piled it with cushions and drapes. It certainly looked more comfortable for the model. She apparently agreed, murmuring a 'thanks' as she placed herself, making minor adjustments before settling.

'Is that okay? Remember it's for forty minutes with a short break half-way through.' He turned to the model. 'Are you quite comfortable?'

She nodded, visibly relaxing in the classic reclining pose.

Peter's position was almost directly in front, making the legs foreshortened and the face in full view. So were the bruises. But now looking even more vivid as the heat of the spotlight had caused the masking make-up to become shiny.

He started to sketch in the form, looking up from time to time. She closed her eyes as though dozing, but once or twice he found them open, looking at him directly. Peter found himself responding with a half-smile, almost conspiratorial, before looking away to concentrate on his emerging drawing. He sensed a presence behind him.

'Not bad,' the tutor said, 'you're definitely getting the feel of it. I see you've brought some pastels, are you going to try a bit of colour?'

'I'd like to. But I'm not sure how to go about it.'

The tutor selected a couple of colours and gently shaded in a small part of the torso.

'Just blend in one or two using the yellow tone and a bit of orange, and some white for highlights. There are no rules really, you can experiment all you like.'

The first half of the session drew to a close. The tutor marked the model's position in chalk on the bottom drape, releasing her from the pose to escape into the cubicle. The students wandered around observing each other's work and making generally positive comments. Usually Peter left the room to avoid this interaction, but today he set out to look at what the easels displayed. In particular he was curious to know whether the bruises were being recorded.

It became the subject of subdued but urgent conversation.

'It doesn't seem right to show her with a black eye.'

'Aren't we supposed to paint what we see?'

'What did the tutor say?'

'He said it's up to me.'

'Well, to me it's like adding further violation to what she's already suffered.' This from an assertive, no-nonsense woman.

'We don't know the circumstances – how can we judge?

Back at his easel, Peter pondered. Yes, he believed she had been a victim. Probably domestic violence, he'd seen plenty of that in his career. Linda used to laugh at his concern for these women, calling him a 'softie'. But she hadn't been a victim. Not then.

He tried a touch of purple and blue to the right eye area and immediately regretted it. Furiously he tried to erase the colour. An ugly mess resulted. I've got a lot to learn, he thought ruefully.

The buzzer sounded. Time was up. The tutor had given him an encouraging nod on his last appraisal without criticising his effort with the pastels. Students were noisily packing up, putting away easels, rolling up the several sheets of their morning's work, preparing to leave.

As they filed out the door, Peter noticed several of them putting coins and even some paper money in the little dish labelled 'model'. Peter felt in his pocket and extracted a fifty-dollar note. He placed it under the others.

The rush of people going down the stairs always felt as though a plug had been pulled. At the front door, Peter realised that the forecast had been right – it was raining. Hard. And he'd left his umbrella behind.

Dashing upstairs he was about to push open the door when the sound of loud voices stalled him.

'I can't get this bloody stuff off. I thought it would wash off easily.'

'If it's greasepaint you used, you have to take it off with cold cream. I know that from my old uni rep days. And by the way, you're quite the little actress, that was all very convincing! Hey, guess what – you've made over seventy dollars! That should get you out of the red, along with your modelling fee.'

'Thanks, Tony. I can't believe I got into so much debt in the first place. Don't tell Mum and Dad, will you. They'd be furious.' Her tone changed. 'I do feel a bit guilty though – people giving me money on false pretences. That quiet bloke sitting on the side – he put in fifty dollars. I was peeping through the curtain and saw it.'

'That's Peter.'

'He looked at me a couple of times with such a kind, sort of understanding expression. I'd say he's a really good person.'

Peter turned to go. He didn't need to hear any more. What a neat little con – fooled him completely. So he'd lost fifty dollars and an umbrella. But he was 'kind' and a 'good person'. Balanced it out, in a way.

For the first time in ages he was smiling as he left the building, thinking how Linda would have had a good old laugh ...

And Dr Roberts surely will.

THE GREEN COAT

The tinny tinkle of a little bell alerted Penny that it was close to closing time at the opportunity shop. She needed to make a choice – maroon or green? Both fitted well, it was really a toss-of-the coin decision. In selecting the green coat, Penny would very soon find that she had significantly changed the course of her future life.

Home, then, to the old miners cottage which was by no means a bargain purchase a year ago, in spite of the global recession.

This country town north of the Great Divide, so accessible to Melbourne by car or train, had become a Mecca for retirees and disenchanted city dwellers. Penny was often asked why she chose Castlemaine – was it the goldmining history, the bush and mountain scenery or the heritage streetscape? She couldn't manage anything more explicit than she liked the look of it when travelling around.

Her return to Rockhampton from England eighteen months ago served only to confirm that she had outgrown her home town and couldn't see herself fitting in there anymore. Whereas, Castlemaine felt 'right.' Penny had no regrets so far. But money was tight, hence the op-shop.

She hung the coat over the back of a chair and glanced at the clock. Nearly half-past-four. Too early for a glass of wine. Okay. She'd wait until five. Sort of a compromise.

Penny looked around the little sitting-room. She often pretended to be seeing it for the first time, allowing features to register as though seeing it through a visitor's eyes. The ceiling was low which added to the cosy feeling. By discarding the worn carpet and restoring the sturdy timber floor, a contemporary country look resulted, enhanced by adding a square light-brown and white fringed woollen rug. The small open fireplace was a big attraction, especially with winter looming, though the cracked tiling surround would need to be replaced in due course.

A low, wooden coffee table in front of the worn, but still comfortable, terracotta-coloured sofa completed the setting. Along the far wall stood a long, well-stocked bookcase, another 'find'. She had brought few personal effects back from England, so it was almost like starting with a clean slate.

On top of the bookcase, a framed photograph of a middle-aged woman stood in isolation. Head and shoulders only, a studio portrait. The gaze was compelling and serious.

Penny allowed herself the luxury of reminiscing every so often. In the grim time after Miranda died she felt she was floundering. Initially, there were the practical issues to attend to, part of the agreed commitment to her friend. After all that, feelings of loss and pointlessness threatened her stability. It was not unlike how she felt when she was cast adrift in London, before she met Miranda. When life with Noel became impossible. How could that have happened? How could she have been so gullible?

Thinking back, she remembered herself in Rockhampton as the rather dumpy, plain but reliable nurse who had become a tutor in the School of Nursing and thought that would be her destiny. Both her older and younger sisters had married and appeared happy, so she was surprised when they warned her about getting serious with the visiting English accountant who had introduced himself to them on a rare girls night out at one of the local pubs. Perhaps he noticed that she didn't wear a wedding ring and decided to concentrate his charm on her. It certainly worked. Penny was flattered and only too eager to believe his compliments were sincere. Probably her sisters were jealous, she thought.

Certainly her parents were impressed with him, especially his double-barrelled name and the plummy accent. When Noel announced to her father that he would have to return to England earlier than he had planned and wanted to take Penny back as his bride, they provided a lavish wedding with all the trimmings one would expect in a provincial Queensland city. Oh, those memories, now more bitter than sweet.

She did not know at the time that Noel had asked for, and received, the sum of five thousand dollars from her father 'to help set up house'. The apartment he took her to fell far short of the glowing description he had given everybody in Rockhampton. It was no more than a cramped one-bedroom flat with primitive cooking facilities and very little storage space.

He changed too. There were no more words of affection and tenderness, in fact quite the opposite. If she made a loving gesture towards him it was repulsed. When she tried to talk to him, ask him what was wrong, he was irritable. 'When am I going to meet your family?' she'd asked timidly one day. 'You wouldn't want to,' was his terse reply.

He became rough and demanding in bed. And critical. 'Don't you know anything about pleasing a man?' he accused. Before long she became aware that he had other love interests, with female voices on the phone asking for him. One of them actually asked her if she was a call-girl. Then he started to not come home at night, and would not divulge his whereabouts to her. 'It's none of your business.'

A rough looking young man knocked on the door one day when he was out. He arrogantly pushed his way in and eyed her up and down. She felt a sense of menace from him, so, stomach muscles contracting, she forced herself to sound neutral: 'Do you want me to give him a message?'

'Yair. Yer can tell him Barry came round for his cut. He'll know what it's about. An' yer can tell him Ralphie's due out soon an' he'll want 'is place back. Din't tell yer about that, did 'e?'

Noel's response to the message was a show of anger. He threw a chair out of his way and swept the dishes off the small table, breaking several. For an instant, from the savage expression on his face, she thought he would hit her. That would be the absolute end if he did. Instead, he went in to the bedroom, slamming the door.

She had never felt so unhappy, lost and lonely. Along with the coldness, both of weather and domestically, Penny found the great city too big and impersonal for her to embrace.

There was only one thing to do – she resolved to look for employment, having always intended to continue her nursing career anyway, though probably not so soon. After all, this was supposed to be her honeymoon. But her short marriage was turning sour. She felt helpless and trapped. Working would at least give her some independence. She had her work permit and good references from Rockhampton Base Hospital to support an application.

Using the phone book as a reference, Penny set about contacting the personnel departments of some of the listed hospitals. This being a totally new experience, her approach was tentative. As well, she found some difficulty in understanding the local accent over the phone. Finally there was a positive response, a vacancy in her area of expertise.

The appointment for an interview at the School of Nursing at Guys resulted in the offer of a position for an initial trial period of three months to teach anatomy and physiology in the student nurse program. At last, something was going right for her.

Things did not improve at home. Noel continued to take every opportunity to belittle her. She had to develop a protective veneer to avoid being hurt. Penny became friendly with other nursing staff at the hospital and let it be known that she would be interested in sharing accommodation if anything became available. This occurred within a month – there was a vacancy near the hospital, in a terrace house shared by two South African nurses and an occupational therapist from New Zealand.

Noel appeared disinterested when she told him she was moving out. She asked if he wanted to speak to her parents about the breakdown of their marriage, to explain his position perhaps. His response was: 'Why should I talk to peasants?' After that, her dislike of him hardened into loathing. She moved out within days.

Her parents were disappointed that the marriage was over after only a few months. They seemed to take the position that it would have been her fault. She didn't tell them of the nastiness she had endured and her suspicions that the charming person they had warmed to was quite a shady character.

The uncontested divorce was finalised the following year. Her sense of failure was mixed with relief. 'I guess I was meant to be an old maid all along,' was her fatalistic attitude.

Her gaze went back to the photograph. It was quite strange, really. She had only known Miranda for about three years, having met after a seminar at Guys Hospital at which Miranda was the keynote speaker. Penny plucked up enough courage to meet her afterwards and to identify herself as a fellow Australian, from Queensland. That led to regular contact and, eventually, to her role in Miranda's last years.

The School of Nursing accepted her request to work on a part-time basis initially, and agreed to her having unlimited unpaid leave when Miranda's need for constant attention became greater.

In a way, it was text-book stuff. No false hopes, just the gradual inexorable decline until the inevitable became a sad, but ultimately welcome release.

The biggest shock was in the reading of the will. Penny was aware of the list allocating personal property to friends and knew that Miranda intended to give bequests to her two nephews and niece.

But when the solicitor had read out: 'The bulk of my estate I leave to my devoted friend Penelope Marsham,' she had been genuinely overwhelmed. The amount, after adjustments, would be in the region of one hundred thousand pounds. Penny had gasped, 'What?'

'I can see you're shocked, Miss Marsham. But I can only tell you that Doctor Shaw was very clear in her instructions. She's left some smaller bequests to organisations with which she was involved and of course some to her family. But she said to me that your care of her was priceless. And I have to agree.'

Penny's mind had reeled. Money had never been a topic of conversation between them, though Penny knew that a professorial salary was substantial and also that there was income generated by Miranda's publications. With the exception of the purchase of the specialised bed for pressure area prevention, as recommended by the oncology department, Miranda didn't seem to spend much money at all. She had said at one stage that there should be enough money to publish her memoirs, 'if you think it's worth doing.'

She looked over at the black box under the window. So far she hadn't felt like opening it up again. The written documents in it contained poignant references to Miranda's personal life, which she had transcribed to Miranda's dictation, along with journals, newspaper articles and two audio tapes. One day it might feel right to begin the task of editing all that material Miranda had left behind.

Resolutely, Penny got to her feet and poured herself a glass of wine. A local red, not bad. A glance at the clock, and awareness of the winter evening light fading, confirmed the passage of time. Nearly six o'clock! That's what ruminating does to you ....

Time to try the coat on again. It fitted really well, two deep pockets, nice big buttons, a classic style. It actually felt like new. Running her hands along the lining she was surprised to find a hidden pocket with something in it. It turned out to be a brown envelope which had been opened. Inside was a postcard-sized sepia photograph of a young man in army uniform. An enclosed slip of paper had the handwritten message: 'I thought you should have this, Dorrie. Esmae.'

Penny looked at the envelope. Impossible to decipher the date on the postmark. The stamp itself looked very old. In the same handwriting as in the note, the address read: 'Miss Dorothy Jessop, 23 Monmot Street, Castlemaine.'

A check of the phonebook did not reveal an entry for D. Jessop, although this was not particularly surprising. Some people did not want their addresses made public. Too late to go in search now. Penny resolved to visit Miss Jessop's address in the morning.

It turned out to be a somewhat weather-beaten timber house up a side street, looking out of place between the well-maintained premises on either side. Penny noted the unkempt garden with children's bikes and toys scattered around. Her knock on the door was eventually answered by a youngish woman carrying a baby aged about six months on her hip, her face showing the grey, resigned expression of chronic lack of sleep. Penny heard at least two other children yelling inside the house.

The woman eyed her. 'Yes?'

'Hello,' said Penny brightly, 'I'm looking for a Miss Dorothy Jessop who used to live here.'

'Well she don't now. Shut up, you two! We've been here since January when His Lordship got his transfer.' Penny must have looked puzzled. 'To the gaol, I mean. Just out of town.'

'Oh, I see. Who would know where Miss Jessop is, then? I've got something that belongs to her.'

'Try the agent. It's the first one in Barker Street. Look, I gotta go before they kill each other. Not that I'd mind,' she added, lips twisting in more of a grimace than a smile.

The girl behind the desk in the real estate agency was helpful. She looked up the file relating to the address. 'This house was sold under instructions from the Public Trustee. The purchaser bought it as an investment, the current tenant is the third.'

'Does that mean she's dead then ?'

'No, not necessarily. She was an old lady, she may have gone into residential care. Perhaps you could ask at the Aged Care office, it's just around the corner. Good luck!'

Penny identified herself at the signposted premises, saying she had something Miss Jessop might appreciate being returned to her.

'Really? I doubt it! The poor old soul is wandering in her mind these days. Anyway, she's in the nursing home attached to the hospital if you want to make contact with her.'

Penny thanked the receptionist and decided to proceed, now that she had a destination. Elmore House was once a stately mansion that had been acquired and refurbished by the Health Department to provide long-term care for the elderly.

She parked in the visitors' car park and rang the bell on the desk in reception. A nursing aide appeared and, in response to Penny's request, went to check if the person in charge was free. Years ago it would have been 'matron', but that rather comforting term was now obsolete.

The notice on the door read: 'Director of Nursing – Gwenda Davis.' That person, a solidly built, grey-haired woman of about fifty, rose from behind her desk to greet her, hand outstretched, smile on her face.

'Do come in. I'm Gwenda Davis. What can I do for you?'

Penny explained her reason for seeking out Miss Jessop and showed her the envelope.

'Well, well! Isn't that interesting! I wonder if he was a relative, or even a boyfriend of Dorrie's. Do sit down, Penny. I'll explain her situation to you.' After getting settled she continued. 'Miss Jessop is a single lady who would have been described as a spinster in the past. As far as we know, she has only one living relative, her brother, a bachelor in his seventies called Bertie Jessop. He lives in a retirement village in Bendigo and visits her once a month. The problem is, Dorrie has dementia, she tends to ramble without anything making any sense.'

'I understand that, Gwenda. I've done my share of geriatric nursing in the past. I know how frustrating it can be.'

'Good. Now, would you like to meet her and give this to her yourself?'

Penny found herself intrigued enough to agree. She followed the senior nurse down the passage, noting the majestic high ceilings and rooms leading off on each side. They appeared to be two-bed or four-bed rooms, neat and empty. In two of the bigger rooms she noticed that one of the beds was occupied with cot-sides in position. She assumed the other residents would be in a day room.

Gwenda paused at a closed door, knocked before opening it, and entered. Penny noted that it was a small room, most of the space being taken up by a single bed. Attending to the person in it was a nursing assistant, a balding man of probably late fifties, who was straightening the bedclothes.

'Oh, Felix – you're fixing Dorrie up. Have you finished?'

'Yes, Mrs Davis. I'm just leaving.'

The diminutive, white-haired elderly person gabbled in an incomprehensible jumble of words. Penny thought she heard 'curr, curr' and 'Yes, yes,' then 'No, no.'

It was really only guess-work. Babbling was the only word for it. The male nurse deftly picked up the bedpan from a chair and left.

'Dorrie has a private room. All the things in here are hers,' Gwenda explained.

Penny recognised a picture of the house in Monmot Street. It could have been from the real estate office, given to her as a memento after the sale. Noticing her interest, Gwenda confirmed what Penny already knew.

'That was her home, she lived there all her life. On her own after her parents died. As far as we know she didn't ever work but looked after her parents until they eventually died. I don't think she belonged to Senior Citizens or anything like that. She was a bit of a recluse really. Anyway, as her health started to fail, she also became quite senile. The health authorities tried using home help and district nurses for a while, but she got to the stage of needing full-time care for various reasons, her safety being one of them. The proceeds from the sale of the house were invested by the Public Trustee and used to pay for her care here, so I'm not breaching confidentiality by telling you this, everybody knows Dorrie, she's been in this town all her life.'

'Is she able to get up and about?' Penny asked.

'Oh yes. We try to get everyone up where possible, but she's quite unsteady on her feet. She had a fall a couple of days ago and the doctor thought she should rest in bed for a while. She gets very confused at times, as you can probably tell. I'm not sure about her eyesight either, but she seems to hear all right.'

During this conversation Dorrie had been restless, plucking at the bedclothes and moving constantly. She kept up her muttering which sounded like 'Come back, come back, curr – dad not here – ahhhh.'

'What is she saying? Can anyone work it out?' Penny asked.

'Sometimes she talks almost sensibly, but she's really rambling at the moment. Having no teeth doesn't help matters. That nurse you just saw, Felix, he seems to be a favourite of hers. He can do anything with her. She can be quite nasty and irritable with other staff, I've seen her fight with them about getting undressed, for example. Look, I'll try to introduce you, but don't be disappointed if she doesn't respond.' Gwenda moved closer, bending down over the cot-side. 'Dorrie – I've got someone here to meet you.'

'Ohhh! Who's this?' Looking rather like a monkey, she squinted up at Penny.

'My name's Penny. It's nice to meet you, Dorrie.'

'Penny? Penny? Don't know any Penny – any penny, any penny. Ohhh!' Her voice became a mumble again. She turned away, yawning cavernously.

'We should let her be, Penny. She's not herself today. She might be in pain, too. I'll check with the nurse in charge to see if she's been ordered anything.' She replaced the cot-side and issued an invitation. 'Come back to the office and have a cup of tea with me.' She smiled at Penny. 'I don't often get to speak to anyone other than staff or relatives.'

Penny found herself chatting comfortably with the older

nurse who encouraged her to elaborate on her recent life story. It helped that Gwenda recognised Miranda's name from some publicity in the past. She showed a genuine interest in hearing about Penny's role in Miranda's terminal illness, and the subsequent return to Australia.

'I've concentrated on getting myself settled, which has been a healing experience in many ways. But I'm too young for the pension and I'll need to think about earning an income soon.'

'Do you want to go back to nursing education? It's all university-based these days, but I'm sure you'd find something in the system.'

'I don't know, Gwenda. Maybe I should look into doing something different, check out training courses or something. I've seen some advertised.'

'Would you consider coming here as a volunteer for a day or two a week? While you're sorting out your possibilities, I mean. There are people here, like Dorrie, who don't have visitors and there aren't enough staff to spare the time to take them out on walks, for example. Or reading to them. One of our chaps is almost blind, but he likes to know what's going on in the world and to talk about it. You'd have to have a police check, but I guess that wouldn't be a problem.'

'Hey, that's a great suggestion,' Penny responded as the idea took hold. 'I really do need to commit myself to something. Getting back to Dorrie – do you happen to know when her brother is due to visit next? I'd like to meet him and show him this photo, perhaps he could shed some light on it.'

'What a good idea!' Gwenda extracted a diary from the filing-cabinet. 'We like relatives to tell us when they plan to come, so we can encourage the resident to prepare for the visit. Those who are alert enough, anyway. Here we are – Bertie's due to see her the week after next. Sunday, June 17 - 2pm, it says here. I'll make a note for the afternoon staff to introduce you to him. I don't work weekends, one of the perks of being boss,' she chuckled, then continued, 'Mind you, the buck stops here!'

Back home, Penny opened her diary to record the entry for the seventeenth and in so doing was reminded that she had guests arriving this coming weekend. Miranda's brother and sister-in-law, Brian and Jo Shaw, were to make their first visit to her, coming up on Saturday and staying overnight. Penny was grateful that in their busy lives they had always showed an interest in her wellbeing with phone calls every six or eight weeks.

What a great couple! Penny's first contact with them was in England when the whole family came over for a month. Miranda had been so insistent on this visit that Brian had suspected that there was an underlying reason. This was confirmed when, at an appropriate time, Miranda had unemotionally disclosed her terminal diagnosis. She had asked Penny to be there as well.

'Hell, Sis! Why didn't you tell us?' Brian had expostulated. Jo registered total shock. Their daughter, Janie, had burst into tears. The two older sons, both in their twenties, seemed to be frozen. Uncharacteristically, Penny had spoken up.

'This is all a terrible shock to you, I can see how you feel. I want you to know that I'm here for Miranda, in whatever way I'm needed.'

Miranda then went on to say that she didn't know how long she had left, but wanted this time together to be very special. 'I didn't want you coming all this way for a funeral. Let's have a good time now instead!' Which is what they did. When the four weeks were up, final goodbyes were said. Everyone was determined to be brave, knowing it was to be the last time.

Immediately after the will had been read, Penny rang Brian in Melbourne to tell him that she was the principal benefactor, but if they wanted to challenge this, she would co-operate.

From over ten thousand miles away Brian's voice was firm and unwavering.

'We knew about that, Penny. Miranda told us what she intended, and we're in complete agreement. Please keep in touch with us. Let us know what you decide to do.'

It would be good to see them again.

Mentally, she checked the arrangements. The spare room was pristine, no problems there. She had a portable halogen heater to warm it up, there was an electric blanket for the sofa bed. Due to their commitments, it was to be an overnight stay only, which meant dinner in the evening, breakfast and lunch the following day.

Late afternoon, the grey Toyota sedan came to a halt in the driveway. Warm greetings, a tour of the property, and afternoon tea in the cosy living room followed.

Jo was enthusiastic. 'I really love what you've got here, Penny! I can see where you've put your own personal touches. Janie would just love it, I know.'

'She would be very welcome, also the boys. What are they doing? Give me an up-to-date report. Is Byron still a lecturer at La Trobe?'

'Oh yes!' Jo replied, 'though a senior lecturer now. He's living up to his name, quite an authority on the Romantic and Victorian poets. He's had a few articles published recently. He certainly didn't get it from me, did he Brian!'

'No, I think he takes after my mum, she always loved literature. Though he never really knew her, he was only a toddler when she died. I remember how thrilled she was when we decided to call him Byron instead of Brian Junior. Actually it would have been Brian the Third as that was Dad's name too. Anyway he's doing okay and going steady with a nice girl.'

Penny smiled at the old-fashioned expression. 'And Stephen? He's the scientist, isn't he?'

'Yes, research at Peter Mac. Not well-paid, but he seems to be really involved. You may remember that he used his inheritance from Miranda to do six months study in the US. He's on his way to his PhD.' There was no hiding the pride in Brian's voice.

Jo took over: 'Janie's in Perth at the moment, staying with my parents. She did her Arts degree but wasn't sure where to go with it. She's working in a bookshop and generally enjoying herself. Mum and Dad love having her, they're really active, even though they're well into their seventies. Janie's now twenty-two. I'm sure in due course she'll find Mr Right.'

'I thought she was pretty keen on that Italian chap,' said Brian.

'No, that's fallen through. Anyway, enough about us – what have you been up to, Penny?'

'Let me just get this casserole heated up and I'll tell you everything after dinner.'

As she busied herself with the meal preparation, Penny explored a twinge she had felt when Jo talked about Janie finding Mr Right. Her own experience had been so painful it had set her on a path of deliberate celibacy for quite a few years. Was this inevitable? Why did other people seem to find their Mister or Miss Right? Was it a fault in her, a deficiency of some sort, or just luck?

No answer was likely to be forthcoming, so she concentrated on providing a tasty, warming meal for her visitors.

Later, relaxing with a glass of port in front of the sparkling log fire, she told them of her find in the op-shop coat pocket, and the mystery it had created.

'I haven't shown it to Dorrie yet. She's so confused it probably wouldn't register with her. I decided to make copies so that if anything happened to the original there would be a replacement.' She gave them each a copy of the old photograph.

'I' m thinking of giving the original to the brother when he comes to visit her next Sunday. It'll be interesting to see if he recognises the person.'

Brian studied the photo closely. 'Tell you what, he looks rather Germanic, doesn't he? Square face, strong jaw.'

Jo agreed, and looking at the copy she held, commented: 'Your father was in the army, wasn't he, Brian ?'

'He was. I was born just after the war ended. He was one of the first to be sent home. He'd suffered pretty badly with dysentery in the tropics and a leg injury which left him with a limp. He never wanted to talk about it, didn't join the RSL or anything. Mum said he had some really bad memories, nightmares I suppose they were, but he didn't ask for any help. Not that there would have been anything available then anyway.'

'Where did he serve?' asked Penny.

'New Guinea.' Brian became reflective. The two women waited for him to continue. 'He tried to be a good dad, I guess he was better with me than with Miranda. He always believed that if an adult told you to do something, you did it. Straight away. Without question. Miranda always wanted to know "why". Mum was constantly trying to keep the peace between them. He was good with our kids, though, wasn't he, Jo?'

'A great grandad!' she agreed, smothering a yawn.

It was not lost on Penny. 'You two must be so tired. Bedtime, eh?'

'It's the fire. And the lovely meal. And ...' She yawned again.

Penny and Brian shared the habit of early rising.

'Jo loves to sleep in, always has,' said Brian.

They sat drinking tea in companionable silence. Brian listened to the late morning continuation of the dawn chorus. 'It's so good to hear the birds. You miss that in Melbourne.'

'Even more so in England. They have their own breeds there, of course, but I really missed the maggies! Brian – did you ever get to read Miranda's memoir notes? They're actually still in draft form.' He shook his head.

'They're in that box over there if you'd like to take a look. I'm just going to nick into town and get the Sunday paper and some fresh rolls for lunch.'

His sister's written thoughts and words were honest, and, for a close relative would be intrinsically poignant. Penny took her time returning from the supermarket to allow him privacy in reading them.

When she returned, Jo was up and dressed, had breakfasted, and was ready to go.

'Are you going to take us on a tour of your adopted town, Penny? I know Brian's been here before. His home town is the other side of those mountains, I think. But I'm from the West and it's all new to me.'

Brian opted to stay behind and re-read Miranda's notes.

'A lot of these memories are mine, too. It's strange to read another person's version, always a detail or two that isn't quite how you remember it. Like Mum's funeral, for example.'

Waving them goodbye a few hours later, Penny relished a pleasing sense of satisfaction. It had been a successful visit for both host and guests. Strange how she felt more at home with them than with her own family.

When she went to Rockhampton, she had made it a point of pride to return the money that Noel had accepted from her parents. Miranda's legacy had enabled this. Initially, she had tried to save the money from her salary, but a few trips with Miranda's family had eaten into it, and of course her unpaid leave from work meant her savings dwindled even more.

'You don't have to, you know,' her father had said stiffly.

It was all too difficult to talk about. Dad had always claimed to be a good judge of character, and in fact said to her: 'You let a good man go.'

When she tried to enlist her mother's understanding of her unhappy experience, she found an equally rigid position. 'You have to work at marriage, you know.' It felt as though everyone blamed her for the failure. As well, snide references to her devotion to Miranda wounded her, making her feel defensive.

She sensed that they were quite relieved when she decided to settle in Victoria, knowing that for them any trip south was unlikely, and would certainly not take place during winter. Queenslanders find it hard to cope with temperatures of less than twenty degrees.

She planned her week. First she would get the copy of the photograph enlarged. A bigger image might help Dorrie see, and maybe remember. It was worth trying anyway. However, she would show Bertie Jessop the original. It seemed the right thing to do.

Both Brian and Jo had approved of the idea of her volunteering at Elmore House. 'You're so kind and patient, you'd be a natural,' Jo had enthused. Penny made an appointment for Wednesday morning.

Mary Kirkpatrick, the co-ordinator for volunteering services, welcomed her in her shoebox of an office in the main hospital building.

'I'm really glad you have decided to help out at the nursing home,' she said. 'I get lots of enquiries for the children's ward, and people want to be tea ladies, or work in the kiosk. Not many choose the oldies, I'm afraid.'

'It may not be for very long, Mary. Sooner or later I'll need to get paid work.'

'I understand that. But for now, let's get you registered. Here's the application for a police check, which is mandatory.

It will take a few weeks to be processed, but you can start at any time, as long as we know it's been applied for. I'll arrange for a name-badge for you, and of course you'll need to sign on and off each time you come, that's a Health and Safety regulation. Do you have any questions?'

'No, it all seems straightforward. I'll pop in and see if Gwenda Davis is around, to let her know I've taken this step. I'm coming up this Sunday to meet a relative of one of the residents, that's an arrangement I've made with her.'

'She's a good sport, is Gwenda. I've known her for years. Well, thanks again for coming along. There'll be something in the post in a day or so to confirm your new role.'

In Gwenda's roomier office, Penny informed the senior nurse that the formalities for volunteering had been dealt with, and she was ready to offer her services. 'How's Dorrie today?' she asked.

'Better. Physically, that is. She has been up, but really needs a carer with her a lot of the time. She's very confused.'

'That male nurse, Felix – you said he is able to manage her.'

'That's true. From the time he first came here she took to him. He's off today, he has Wednesdays and Sundays off. She always seems a bit lost when he's not around. Anyway, your work will be with all the residents. Would you like to meet a few of them now since you're here?'

Penny followed her into the large community room and was introduced to several of the aged residents. She privately marvelled at the realisation that behind each of the grizzled and time-worn countenances there would be an individual life story going back over many decades. Their history would be that of the nation at war: the First and Second World Wars, the Korean conflict, the reign of Robert Menzies, outside lavatories, large families, the White Australia policy. Random examples of the past came to mind.

Some of these elderly people might have been born overseas with their own issues of survival. What a wealth of experiences, sorrows and joys were now, for many, not accessible, she thought, with a feeling of regret. Memory loss, speech difficulties and confusion would each contribute to this situation.

Leaving the nursing home, Penny felt that she had made a connection which could add some tangible purpose to her life. Her next visit would be on Sunday, with the prospect of meeting Dorrie's brother and perhaps solving the mystery of the identity of the young man in the photograph.

Until then there was plenty to do domestically. Even in midwinter there were gardening jobs to be tackled, especially some late pruning. It felt good to feel the soil between her fingers, deal with emergent weeds, and plan the veggie patch. This was a special challenge. The years she had spent in London meant no gardening at all. Before that, she had lived in sub-tropical central Queensland, so being here in north-central Victoria meant there was much to learn. She leaned heavily on any local knowledge generously provided by the plant nurseries in the town.

A rose bush was her very first planting. It held pride of place in the small flower garden, a tribute to Miranda who had exclaimed with delight at a bunch Penny had once brought her: 'Peace! It's my favourite! How did you know?' The bush looked strong and healthy. In summer, the yellow, pink-tinged flowers would refresh the memory of the friendship. These intangibles keep me going, Penny thought. It's good to have the responsibility of caring for this special place where I've put down roots.

Sunday finally arrived. Penny made her way early to wait in the reception area. A little after two she saw a taxi pull up, and an elderly man, short and stooped, emerged. Penny was about to move forward to meet him when the afternoon charge nurse came down the corridor.

'How do you do!' she said to Penny, offering her hand. 'You must be Miss Marsham. I'm Robyn Jones. Let me introduce Mr Jessop to you.'

The elderly man turned to look at Penny, a bit nonplussed. What was this about?

Robyn Jones explained: 'Miss Marsham has met your sister and would like to talk with you. Also, I believe she has something to show you both.'

Bertie Jessop said nothing, though his lips seemed to move in a soundless, 'How do you do.' He then set off on the familiar path to his sister's room, Penny following. Dorrie was in bed with the cot-sides in place, somewhat curled up and appearing to be dozing.

'Dorrie, wake up! It's me, it's Bertie. Wake up!'

She stirred, moved in his direction and opened her eyes.

'Bertie? Bertie's me big brother! Bertie's naughty! Bertie's naughty!' she carolled in a sing-song voice.

'Yes, it's me. I'm here. Can you see me?'

She started to cackle, sounding like a half-laugh which appeared to irritate him. He drew a chair up to the bed and motioned Penny to do the same.

'I don't know why I bother. It's a waste of time.' He turned toward the younger woman and fixed his pale eyes on her. 'What did you want to show her?'

'This all came about when I bought a coat, which obviously belonged to your sister, at a secondhand shop. I know this because I found this in an inside pocket and was able to track her down. But she seems too confused for me to actually give it to her, so I thought you might be able to help.'

She handed him the envelope watching as he carefully opened it. He took out the note and the photograph. There was an immediate change in his demeanour. He glared at the photo with a look of intense dislike.

'That – that scum! That stinking German scum!' he hissed.

Penny was taken aback at his vehemence. It was totally unexpected.

'You – you know who it is, then?'

'Of course I do. I could never forget that face. It's that mongrel Kurt Schroeder! He ruined Dorrie's life, and he ruined mine! I hate him! I'm glad he's dead!'

Penny chose her words carefully. 'Was he someone special to Dorrie? A sweetheart perhaps?'

Bertie Jessop let out a deep breath through his teeth. Penny wasn't sure whether he would answer or not. Eventually he decided to continue.

'He was the rat who ruined all our lives.'

'Don't go on if it's painful for you.' Penny's voice was gentle. Dorrie twisted around in her bed seemingly oblivious to her visitors.

'It was so long ago it shouldn't matter anymore. He's dead. Tom's dead. Dad and Mum are long dead, and she might as well be dead.' His voice trailed off.

After a pause, Penny ventured: 'What was she like as a young girl?'

'Oh, full of spirit she was. Too much for her own good. This – this person,' he spat the word, 'came into Dad's hardware store one day when she was behind the counter. It must have been after school. She would have been about sixteen. He took a fancy to her and came back a lot. Dad didn't approve when he found out, because of the German name. He was dead against the Krauts because of the First World War. Lost family members over there. Anyway, when Dorrie said she wanted to go out with him, he said no. Mum didn't say anything, she never did. Wasn't allowed to.'

He paused for a moment. Penny thought he probably wasn't used to talking much. She was prepared to be patient.

'Then he – that Kurt – got his call-up papers. He was born in Australia, but his parents had migrated here. Lutherans, they were. Dorrie was real worried that he was going away to fight and might get killed. She arranged for him to come around one night to tell my father that they wanted to get married. Because of her age, he would have to give permission. There was a terrible scene – I remember it well. How could I ever forget! Dad hit the roof. "No, –," he used a strong swear word, "Kraut is going to marry a daughter of mine!" Then this Kurt got on his high horse, and I thought they would come to blows. But it was worse than that.'

He stopped and appeared to be debating whether to continue. Penny silently willed him to go on.

'He turned to me and said loudly and nastily: "At least I'm a proper man, not like your poofter of a son!"'

'Dad was thunderstruck. "What are you talking about, you mongrel?" he yelled. "The only wife he'll ever have is his best mate, Tom." He spat the words at me. I don't know how he knew, he just did. Probably Dorrie told him, she caught us kissing a couple of times when we thought we were alone. It changed everything in our family. I was only nineteen, but I knew Tom and I were meant to be together.'

His voice became softer and reflective. 'And we were. For all those years. He died five years ago, come September.'

It wasn't hard to imagine the difficulties they would have confronted in that long relationship. Homophobia was part of the ingrained culture, especially in the country. Perhaps they had experienced a grudging acceptance over time. Penny didn't dare ask. Her heart went out to this faded old man.

'And Dorrie? What happened to her?'

'They did a midnight flit. No-one heard anything for

months, over a year. Then she turned up again. There had been an accident at the army barracks in Townsville and he'd been killed. So she came back home. But not for long.'

He paused significantly. 'They sent her away again. To a – a home in Melbourne. She was a different person when she came back. It was like her spirit had been broken.'

'Are you saying she had given birth to a child? '

'Yes. A bastard. If she'd kept it she would have been an unmarried mother. With all the shame that would have caused.'

'So the baby was adopted out?'

'Presumably. My parents didn't even want to know whether it was a boy or girl. I don't know whether Dorrie did either. Mum might have wanted to know, but Dad would have over-ruled her. It would have been their only grand-child as things turned out. Dorrie was ordered to carry on as though nothing had happened. She was told to talk to no-one, no-one at all. She was never allowed to forget how sinful she had been.'

'Poor Dorrie. What a sad story – she lost so much.'

'I blame him! He walked all over us! I have never hated anyone as much as ....' He suddenly grabbed the photograph and savagely tore it to pieces. 'I hope you are rotting in hell, you bastard !'

'I'm sorry I've managed to rake it all up again.' Penny felt genuinely remorseful, but had one further question. 'Tell me – who is this Esmae?

'I don't know. Maybe someone from the home. That envelope looks old. She must have had it for years.' His voice now sounded flat and tired.

A volunteer pushing a tea-trolley appeared at the door.

'Cuppa, anyone?' she asked cheerily.

Penny shook her head. Bertie mumbled 'No, thanks.' Dorrie appeared to have dozed off again. There was a somewhat uneasy silence.

'Mr Jessop, I think it's wonderful that you make the effort to come and see your sister. I can see it can't be much fun for you. I'm going to be a volunteer here for a few months. I want you to know I will keep a close eye on her, as far as I can. She seems to be quite a favourite here.' The last bit may not have been strictly true, but she thought it might reassure him.

'Oh yes,' he said diffidently, 'people always protect her - I was cut off, you know. Not a penny. Still, at least I can look after myself, and I've got all my marbles.' He sat for a minute. 'I think I'll go now.'

Penny offered to drive him to the station, but he declined, saying he would order a taxi from reception.

'I won't be a hypocrite and say it was nice to meet you, given what you brought up. At least you know her story now. I'd be grateful if you didn't broadcast it around. Let her keep a bit of dignity. If that's possible.'

Back home, Penny resolved to write down as much as she could while it was fresh in her mind. It was such a poignant story. How different things were in those days. If only Dorrie could talk and share her memories. But dementia doesn't allow for any recovery, she knew that. What she had found out was probably all that would ever be available.

One thing, though – she couldn't wear that green coat now. It wouldn't feel right. She decided to put it in Dorrie's wardrobe. The old lady might even get to wear it again when the weather was warm enough for residents to venture outside.

Mary Kirkpatrick phoned on Thursday morning to ask Penny if she could start at Elmore House that afternoon, as one of the regulars had called in sick. She apologised for the short notice. Penny readily agreed, and in due course found her way to the staff-room to leave her belongings. One of the staff gave her an apron. In large letters she wrote 'PENNY' with a marker on a peel-off sticker as temporary ID.

'This will do until your proper name tag arrives. Now, Mr Drake likes to have a game of draughts – are you up for that?'

'He'll probably beat me, I'm really out of practice,' Penny laughed. After six games he was well ahead, and decided to watch television instead. Probably less boring, Penny thought ruefully.

Before long it was time for preparation for the evening meal. Staff moved with practised routine, escorting individual residents to the toilet, then settling them at their usual places at the table and generally assisting with food delivery.

The bedridden usually needed to be fed, either by a staff member, a relative or a volunteer. The vitamised or semi-solid meals looked uninteresting, but Penny knew they contained essential nutrients. Few of the residents had many natural teeth left, and, for some, dentures no longer fitted properly in slack jaws with shrunken soft tissue.

'Who's looking after Dorrie?' she asked.

'Oh Felix, I expect. He's her favourite. We don't mind, it's not a competition.'

'I'll just pop in and say hello.'

Sure enough, the male nurse was encouraging her to eat.

'Come on, Dorrie, one more mouthful.'

'Curr, curr!' she spluttered. 'Come on, curr!'

He was surprised to see Penny, but relaxed when she smiled at him.

'She's calling you Kurt!'

'I know, she always does, it must mean something to her.'

He put the bowl and spoon down on the tray. In the instant his right hand was free, Dorrie seized it, pulling it down under the bedclothes to her pubic area.

'Ohh, nice, nice!'

Felix extricated his hand and shot an embarrassed look at Penny.

'She's – what do you call it? – disinhibited.' He sounded each syllable separately, as though the word was unfamiliar.

He wiped her lips with a napkin, put the cot-side up and made ready to leave.

'How do the others manage her?'

'She's not like that with anyone else, only with me. But I can cope.'

Back home, Penny discovered a small envelope in her mailbox. The postie had been late again. It was a 'Thank You' note from Jo Shaw. Along with the words of appreciation was a comment from Brian saying how impressed he was with the draft notes of Miranda's memoirs. Penny had a premonition that there may be more to come in that regard.

She found herself thinking more about Dorrie and the story her brother had provided. The 'curr–curr ' sound she persisted in now seemed almost certainly to refer to 'Kurt Schroeder,' her lover. She checked her rough notes, not sure of the exact spelling. Not that it really mattered. So this male nurse had become part of Dorrie's fantasy. Harmless enough, she reasoned.

So far, she hadn't divulged what she had learned from Bertie Jessop to anyone. Probably when she saw Gwenda Davis again she would be asked the outcome of the meeting with Dorrie's brother. She would say, quite truthfully, that he identified the person in the photo as someone he didn't like and tore it up. End of story. But there were some tantalising loose ends. The coat, for example. How and when did Dorrie get it? Was it bought with the help of one of her carers? Was the photo in the envelope the only connection she had with her long-lost lover?

Penny experienced a familiar sense of personal privilege. It had been something to treasure when Miranda had chosen her to record her memories. Now she had information which may lead on to understanding another person's life. Or perhaps not. What she knew now might be all that is ever going to be available.

Be practical, you silly girl, she admonished herself. Get on with it, do your housework, keep an open mind.

Her next session of volunteer work at Elmore House was to be Saturday afternoon. 'We're especially grateful to anyone who can volunteer on weekends,' Mary had said. 'Most people have family commitments then.' Yes, most people do.

The phone rang. It was the manager of the camera shop saying her photo order was ready. She arranged to pick it up on Monday when she did her shopping and also had a GP appointment. This time she hoped he would agree to her coming off the antidepressant she'd been taking since Miranda died. She would explain that she didn't need it now that she had put down roots, and had some structure to her life.

Saturday was cold and windy. Surprisingly, in spite of the high ceilings, Elmore House was well heated. It was good to be able to recognise some of the staff now. She settled readily into the routine, being particularly alert to the needs of the non-verbal residents. She asked after Dorrie and was told she had been up earlier but had gone back to bed after lunch.

Staff on duty took turns to have their afternoon tea. During her break in the staffroom, Penny asked whether the nursing home continued to look after those residents who became terminally ill, or were they transferred to the General Hospital.

'They stay here unless surgery is required, which is, of course, a medical decision. Most often, though, they slip into a coma and we do whatever care is necessary. It's a lot to do with quality of life and their own wishes.' Penny nodded. It was what she had expected. Miranda hadn't wanted to go into hospital at the end either, and everyone respected that choice.

'See you all on Tuesday. I'll look in on Dorrie on my way out.'

Again, Felix was dealing with her, his back to the partly opened door.

What she saw made her stop in her tracks in disbelief. The male nurse was embracing the old lady in what could only be described as an intimate and familiar manner. Then, to Penny's horror, he kissed her lovingly on the lips.

'What are you doing?' Her words brought an abrupt halt to his actions.

Looking shamefaced, he managed to say: 'It's not – it's not what you think! Please don't report this – I can explain!'

Penny's first impulse was to say: 'Of course I have to report it! But the stricken look on his face made her reconsider.

'I – I'll have to think about it. Look, there are some things I know, that you don't.'

He looked bewildered and quite distressed.

'Are you rostered on duty on Tuesday afternoon?' He nodded. 'I'm due back then too. Why don't we meet beforehand, let's say one o'clock. We need to talk.'

He was visibly relieved and muttered 'thanks' as he replaced the cot-side and went out quickly.

The events of the past few days preoccupied Penny to the exclusion of everything else. Foremost on her mind was the scene she had just witnessed which shocked her. This time Felix – she hadn't been told his surname – was clearly participating in an act which would result in suspension, or even dismissal, if it were reported. He would know the strict code forbidding any improper relations with people in care. It would be her duty to inform the management of what she had witnessed.

So why was she hesitant? If it were a case of a member of staff taking advantage of a vulnerable person for his (or her) gratification, she would not hesitate. However, it was not clear that Dorrie was a victim. Far from it. She seemed to actively seek intimacy with this chosen nurse. Penny was certain that she imagined that he was her lover, Kurt. But why would Felix enter into this delusion? Most people, she thought, would find it distasteful. She had read somewhere about the condition of co-dependency – was this the situation here?

Penny knew she would have to put this to him frankly at their meeting on Tuesday. And his response would determine whether she would make a verbal, and, if necessary, a written statement of what she had witnessed.

Yes, it was important to make notes of what happened with times and dates. She added another page to what she had already recorded from the meeting with Bertie Jessop.

She reflected on that meeting and the glimpse it had given her of the drama of almost sixty years ago. She considered the ramifications of Bertie's exposure which would have made him ineligible for military service, according to the rules of the armed forces at that time. Had he already been rejected as 'unfit' due to his sexual orientation and not confessed this to his father? Or had he concocted some other factor to exclude himself from the 'call-up'. The tension in that household must have been unbearable.

She tried to imagine what it must have been like for the parents. So rigid in their outlook, so sure they were right, especially the father. Both of their children became lost to them, in a sense. What bitterness they must have felt, what sadness.

The GP appointment was at 10am on Monday. Penny, as was her habit, arrived ten minutes early and accepted a thirty minute wait. Dr Millar was warmly welcoming.

'You look so much better than last time I saw you,' he remarked after checking her blood pressure as a routine. 'I had been worried about you, your grieving seemed to be quite prolonged. But now you seem to have more energy. So what's been happening ?'

Penny explained about the changes that had occurred in her life, beginning with the chance discovery of the photograph and ending with her becoming a volunteer at the nursing home. She did not reveal the current issue she was concerned about.

'That's good news,' he commented. 'Now, you asked about coming off the antidepressant – I'd like you to do it gradually. Reduce it to one capsule every second day for a month. Come back to see me then. Is that all right?' It was more or less what Penny had expected.

When she called to collect the photograph at the camera shop, she gasped with amazement at seeing the enlargement, which caused the manager to ask anxiously whether there was anything wrong.

'No, no! It's become so lifelike!' Kurt Schroeder's face was much more clearly revealed. In the small sepia original, any similarity was easily overlooked. Now, looking at the blown-up version, Penny immediately knew why Dorrie responded to Felix in the way she did. The resemblance, allowing for age difference, was uncanny.

Tuesday morning arrived. Penny was conscious of a sense of expectation that something very significant was about to be revealed. She was also aware that Felix would have had an uncomfortably anxious wait for their meeting this afternoon.

Sunny day, though still winter cold. It might be a good idea to meet outside in the garden shelter.

What if he doesn't turn up? But no cause for alarm there. As she parked in the volunteer's allocated space she could see him standing in the reception area. She hadn't taken any particular notice of him prior to now. He resembled any other middle-aged man, thickening around the waistline, well-built, strong probably. And there was definitely that squareness of the jaw, 'Germanic', as Brian had described it.

She checked her handbag. All the notes were there, as well

as the copy of the small original and the enlarged portrait of the soldier's face. Time now for sharing information. Only then could she decide on the action she should take.

No-one was behind the desk in reception, so she nodded to Felix and suggested they move out to the gazebo.

'We haven't really been introduced – my name is Penny Marsham. Please call me Penny.'

'Thank you. I am Felix Kranz.'

He watched her intently as she extracted the material from her handbag.

'I'm going to tell you the whole story of my involvement with Dorrie, and what I've been told by her brother. I believe you should be told. However, Mr Jessop insisted that he did not want this to become public knowledge. You will understand why when I explain. Are you okay with that? It's between us. At this stage anyway.'

He nodded and sat forward, listening closely as the story unfolded. When it came to the photograph being torn up, he sighed, disappointment showing on his face. Penny then took out the enlargement and offered it to him.

Never before had Penny seen a man so moved. Tears sprung into his eyes and ran unchecked down his cheeks.

'Thank you, oh thank you! I never ever knew what he looked like,' he gulped.

'Your father?'

He nodded, struggling to regain composure. Several minutes passed.

'Do you think you could explain to me how you came to get here, to work I mean?' Penny asked gently.

'I'd – I'd like to tell you, I will tell you everything. But just now I'm feeling, uh, shattered. But very grateful,' he hastened to add.

'I can see how much of a shock all this is to you. But it

completely explains the bond between you and Dorrie. The trouble is, she thinks you are Kurt, and you can see how she responds.' Penny tried to lighten the tension with a smile.

'I only ever did what she wanted me to – I did it out of love, which I couldn't tell anyone about.'

'Look, I do understand. But there have to be some changes if you want to stay on here – I presume you do ?'

He nodded emphatically. 'It's taken me a long time to find her. I don't want to have to leave her now.'

Penny was thinking hard. A solution which might work came to her mind.

'Felix, how about we both go and see Gwenda Davis? I'll do the talking if you like. I'll say you've confided in me about Dorrie's disinhibition towards you and how this embarrasses you. I would ask her to see if her GP could order a tranquilliser or something to suppress her, well, inappropriate libido.'

'Yes, something like that might help. Might calm her down.'

'That way you've identified the behaviour, and you may get some sympathy, too.'

He fell silent again. Penny asked: 'Is something wrong ?'

'It's the story. It's what she went through. She wasn't given any choice. At least, from the way you've described it, I was a love child. I never even knew that.'

Penny stood up. 'Why don't we see Gwenda now and get the ball rolling before your shift starts. I think she's working today. And Felix – I would really love to hear about your own life. If you wanted to tell me, of course.'

She paused, then took a gamble. 'Would you like to come to my place for dinner, say, Saturday night? That's if you're free, of course. I don't know your personal circumstances. But if you are able, we could have a meal and a good talk.'

Felix's face broke into a wide smile. 'I can't think of anything nicer! I'm on morning shift, but I'm free after that. I really appreciate your invitation. Thank you. I have a lot to thank you for.' He started to choke with emotion but managed to control himself as they made their way to the Director of Nursing's office.

'I'm officially still at lunch, but do come in.' She indicated the armchairs, inviting them to sit down.

Penny initiated the conversation by describing the meeting with Bertie Jessop and his identification of the person in the photograph which he subsequently tore up.

'But the significant thing is that he gave a name: Kurt Schroeder. And that's what Dorrie's saying, especially when Felix is around. That "cur–cur" is actually her saying "Kurt-Kurt!" She thinks Felix is him!'

'It is embarassing,' added Felix, ' and leads her to, well, inappropriate behaviour.'

Gwenda had listened with interest and agreed to raise the issue with Dorrie's GP. She made a point of thanking them both for speaking up about such an awkward situation which had the potential to be misinterpreted.

During the afternoon shift, Penny found herself sensitised to Felix's presence. She observed his caring approach to all of the residents, not only to Dorrie. This seemed to validate her intuitive assessment that he had good qualities. She also realised that she needed to justify to herself the impulsive invitation she had issued. It had certainly been out of character.

Saturday evening at the appointed time, the ring on the doorbell announced his arrival. 'Smart casual' would aptly describe his attire, quite a change from the usual white nursing aide uniform, while the bottle of quality red wine he proffered, struck exactly the right note.

Penny had enjoyed planning this meal. It was good to have someone to prepare for instead of it being just for herself. Over dinner, the conversation stayed light in tone. Both of them were relative newcomers to Castlemaine, each exploring options for community involvement. Felix had joined a local bushwalking group which he enjoyed, when his shifts allowed. Penny said she was toying with learning some craft skills such as mosaic or leadlighting, skills she could use to enhance her home. Each had been divorced with no lingering regrets.

Felix brought up the subject of loneliness. People often seem to expect being alone to be a problem. Penny agreed that it was often put to her that her life must be empty without having a partner.

'To be honest, I just accepted that it might be my destiny. But I'm not antisocial,' she hastened to add.

Felix laughed. 'That is really obvious. You seem to respect and understand people whoever they are. It's an admirable quality.' Penny felt a sense of warmth at his words. He had also said some nice things about her little home. As they moved from the table he examined her bookshelves.

'You've got some of my favourite authors. Some locals, too.'

They sat companionably facing the fireplace with its red glowing logs emitting a steady warmth, each nursing a glass of the excellent red wine Felix had brought.

'That was a delicious meal, Penny! It's been a long time since I've enjoyed eating so much.'

After checking that he liked classical music, and Beethoven in particular, she put a CD of the later piano sonatas on the player. As the rich notes surrounded them, she sat back and looked at her guest expectantly.

'What are your earliest memories?' she asked.

'The couple I called Mum and Dad, and still did even when I knew differently. They were an older couple who wanted children, but it didn't happen naturally for them. They were good people, Mavis and Fred. His name was actually Friedrich, but he changed it, partly because of the anti-German sentiment that was around then. They were Lutherans, Mum joined the church on marriage. They were part of the community up near Horsham. Dad had a small farm, but when it came time for me to leave school he said I should look for a trade, as there wasn't enough income generated by the farm to provide a future for me.'

'How did you feel about that?

'Okay, I guess. I wanted to see more of life anyway. It was a bit quiet where I grew up. Kids left school at fifteen, unless they wanted further education. Not many did. I went down to Ballarat to do an apprenticeship with the Railways. I had to board with a cousin of Mum's.'

'And you didn't know you were adopted?'

'No. Auntie Joan let the cat out of the bag one day when she said: "Getting you kept their marriage together." She was talking about Mavis and Fred. But she'd said "getting" instead of "having". So, being curious, I asked: "Where did they get me from?" She was horrified. "Haven't they told you? Oh, I'm sorry. Forget what I've just said."

'She refused to say another word on the subject.

'Next time when I went home, I asked Mum about it, but was smart enough to begin with, "You're my mother and I love you," which of course startled her. Not my usual turn of phrase! "Please tell me," I begged, "it won't change the way I feel about you and Dad."'

Penny refilled their glasses. He took a few sips before continuing.

'So the information came out, but only on the promise that I didn't take it any further. "See yourself as being chosen," was her advice. The information was scanty anyway. An unmarried mother had especially asked for a Lutheran couple to adopt her child. Mavis thought the Home had closed down, many did in the 60s and 70s.' He paused, holding on to that memory.

'I don't want to bore you with details, so I'll cut the story short. It didn't bother me too much back then. I didn't finish that apprenticeship, I left and joined the police force.'

Penny smiled to herself. This did not surprise her. Felix had that air of competence and authority she always associated with members of the police force.

'My career has been interesting, I worked in several different areas which I can tell you about some other time. As I told you earlier, my marriage didn't last, but I accepted that. I was dedicated to my job, which is sometimes hard for a partner to understand.' They listened to the magnificent sounds of Sonata Number 31.

'And your parents, Mavis and Fred?'

'They were sorry to have not had grandchildren. But they were proud of me as I gained promotion and some good publicity. I think their twilight years were happy enough. I took early retirement to come back and look after them. No way would they have left the farm.'

'So, you did what Dorrie did.'

'I suppose I did. I took the appropriate courses in caring at TAFE in Horsham so I could handle it. Aged Services provided me with respite so I could have an occasional break away, and toward the end, there were two carers who stayed at the farm, one during the day, the other overnight. My parents died within a month of each other, peacefully, I'm glad to say. After that, I started researching my origins, not sure if there were any birth relatives still alive. Eventually I tracked Dorrie down here. I was able to join the staff, thanks to a favourable reference from the GP who looked after Mum and Dad. I think Gwenda was impressed that a son was able to do most of the care of ageing parents.'

'Now you know you've actually got two blood relatives – a birth mother and an uncle.'

'Yes. I haven't yet met him because I always have Sundays off. I'll have to make some decisions about him, I'm not sure what the right thing to do is. Probably nothing at the moment. Especially after what you've told me.'

Penny, recalling the implacable attitude Bertie had taken, nodded.

'You know, Penny, my big regret is that I didn't start the search earlier, before Dorrie became demented. As it is, she will never know that her son is helping care for her.'

The CD came to an end. Penny changed the control over to radio. Classic FM music became the background to their conversation.

'Felix, you don't work on Sundays. Do you want to tell me why not?'

He laughed. 'You would have made a good detective, Penny, you don't miss anything, do you! I'll have to try to phrase this so you don't think I'm a religious nut. As I told you, I had a Lutheran upbringing. But, of course, like for most people, church-going falls by the wayside as you get into the challenges of your career and everything else. Though the values don't really leave you. I didn't realise that until much later. Anyway, when I went back to the farm, I got to speaking to the pastor who came out to minister to my parents. I decided to attend the church services, and still do. For that I go to Bendigo. It's very much a personal thing, people don't always understand that. I'm not trying to impose my beliefs on others.'

Penny sat quietly, considering what she had heard. The pieces of the jigsaw had fallen into place, more or less. Felix Kranz now had a birth history, as well as his actual one. All in all, she decided, he was a most interesting person.

'I don't know how to show you how grateful I am to you.' His voice was serious.

Penny smiled. In the sparkle of the firelight, her face took on a glow of satisfaction and well-being. It's not gratitude I want from you, she thought happily. You have given me a glimpse of a possibility of a future.

'Actually – it's the other way round!'

Realisation slowly dawned on the older man's kindly face.

'You don't mind that I'm, well, quite a lot older than you? I would like to get to know you better. So far it's been all about me, I'm really conscious of that.' He seemed a little apprehensive as he waited for her response.

'The first answer is no, age is not important to me. It's the person who matters, to use that boring cliché. And yes, it would be great to share more of our experiences.' She glanced up at the clock. 'Felix, do you know it's midnight already?'

'What? So it is! I'd better go before my car turns into a pumpkin!'

'I hope you enjoyed the ball!' replied Penny, entering into the spirit of fantasy.

'I won't kiss you goodnight, much as I want to. We probably both need a bit of time to think about what's happened. Would you like to come out to dinner with me next Saturday? There are several great restaurants in Castlemaine. Though none as good as this one, of course!'

A warm handshake and he was gone. To mark the significance of this 'night to remember,' Penny circled the date on her wall calendar. More accurately, it was less of a circle, more of a heart.

Early one morning several weeks later, there was a call from Brian Shaw. It was not totally unexpected, Penny realised.

'Penny,' he asked, 'Would you mind very much if we took over the material about Miranda? I'll tell you why. Byron found a notice in one of the literary journals asking for submissions about the life of Australian women who had made a contribution to humanity. There's some sort of competition being launched. He thought Miranda fell into that category and mentioned it to Janie. Well, you won't believe this – she took to the idea with such enthusiasm that she's come back from Perth and wants to work on it. Miranda was always her "amazing aunt", as she used to put it. Byron would oversee the process, but it depends on you. You might want to do it yourself.'

Miranda experienced a huge sense of relief.

'Brian, I'm so pleased you've rung! What a wonderful opportunity! And absolutely right that her family should take it on board. I'll help in any way I can, of course. I'll send this material to you right away. By registered post,' she added, a smile in her voice.

'Penny, how can we thank you? I'm so grateful, we all are. You'll certainly be acknowledged as a source, or however they put it.'

After he had hung up, Penny laughed to herself. People are always thanking me, she thought. It wasn't necessary. In fact the presence of that box had been silently stirring her conscience for some time. Sending it off was the right thing to do. Gave it the chance of a life in loving hands.

Funny how she had always been the listener to other people's stories. Like being on the outside looking in. As though her own life had been unremarkable, of no interest to anyone. 'Had been' was the operative expression though. Not now, she thought happily, as she searched for sturdy wrapping paper. Her new job at the hospital was due to start soon. Part-time suited her well and the salary was about right. She could stay at Elmore House as a volunteer, maybe just one shift a week.

Sometimes she imagined the events to come: Dorrie's death, whenever that might be. Then, after that happened, Felix's desire to find his father's grave in Townsville, and, if possible, to establish the circumstances of his death. She would be part of that, they had already explored the possibility.

She looked at the clock. The parcel would have to wait until this afternoon. It was nearly time to meet Felix at the Octagon to go on to the bushwalk at Taradale. Walking boots, a light, waterproof jacket, small backpack with a water bottle.

Penny always got her priorities right these days.